Risk vs. Reward

Written by
Preach

Risk vs. Reward
Copyright ©2018 Preach

ISBN 978-1506-907-56-7 PBK
ISBN 978-1506-907-57-4 EBK

LCCN 2018966478

November 2018

Published and Distributed by
First Edition Design Publishing, Inc.
P.O. Box 17646, Sarasota, FL 34276-3217
www.firsteditiondesignpublishing.com

ALL RIGHTS RESERVED. No part of this book publication may be reproduced, stored in a retrieval system, or transmitted in any form or by any means — electronic, mechanical, photo-copy, recording, or any other — except brief quotation in reviews, without the prior permission of the author or publisher.

This book is dedicated to all the women who have been looking for the ultimate man to love, honor and cherish them in every way.

CHAPTER 1

Chance Meetings

It was a Sunday night in 1995; Blake was heading to Rockville for his basketball game. Blake had joined a men's league ten years ago at the request of a co-worker Tim, who was looking for an extra player to complete the roster. Blake, being a former All-American High School and College star was thrilled at playing the sport which gave him the most joy. Traveling to the game, Blake would normally drive to the Anacostia subway stop, located in southeast Washington, DC. This particular night he decided to catch the train at Metro Center, downtown. His plan was to stop and have drinks after the game. As Blake waited on the platform for the train to come, he noticed a very attractive woman standing to his left; her eyes seemingly glued to him as the train approached. Blake boarded the train and took a seat directly across from the woman.

As the train began going through each tunnel, Blake, a very confident man who stands 6 feet 2 inches with broad shoulders and a smile to make butter melt, decided to put the moves on his new admirer. As Blake began to stare at the features of this woman, he noticed she had the most incredible legs he had seen in a long time. Her face was like Chante Moore with a body that the brothers liked to call "PHAT to death". After taking all this in, Blake noticed the seat next to her was unoccupied, so he decided to go over.

"Hello, I'm Blake," he said, while extending his hand. She responded in a low, but sexy voice, "I'm Stacey, nice to meet you Blake." Blake had always been taught by his mother to be direct when talking to people and to be a gentleman especially when talking to women. Keeping this in mind he was confident enough to say, "You have some gorgeous legs." "Thank you," Stacey replied. "No. Thank you!" Blake said with a lusting sigh. "Where are you headed, Stacey?" "I'm going to Mazza Gallery to do some window shopping. What about you?" she replied. "I have a basketball game in Rockville," he responded with a deep baritone voice. "You go all the way to Rockville to play basketball?" asked Stacey. "I actually play in a winter league. I've been playing with the same group of guys for ten years or so. Playing on my end of town can sometimes be hazardous to one's health," he jokingly stated. "What do you mean?" she asked, intrigued by his comment. "I live in southeast, and the guys in the neighborhood take the game a little seriously." Stacey laughed because she knew exactly what he meant. "So, what are you trying to get from the mall?" asked Blake, "I'm just window shopping," she said with a gentle smile that made her entire face light up. Blake, realizing that Stacey's stop would come soon, decided he had to hurry and go for the 'kill'. "Stacey, since you're just window shopping, how about going to the game with me tonight?" Stacey, stunned by his request, was speechless for a second. After a brief pause, she said "Sure, I'll go to your game with you." By this time, Stacey was seemingly having some intimate thoughts of her own. "Damn, he's fine as shit! Give me an hour maybe even two"…Stacey thought to herself.

Her first thought was that she must be crazy. She didn't even know this guy and to make it worse, she had never done anything like this. Why did she allow her stop to go by and not get off the train? What was it about him that made her say yes? Was it his wonderful smile, him being gentleman-like, his sexy voice or maybe she was horny and curious. She didn't know the answers to her questions yet, but something within told her to take a chance. She secretly hoped he wasn't some crazed maniac or rapist. The next few hours would tell her a lot.

As they journeyed, seemingly surprised at the other, it appeared that their chance meeting and, even more, the chance they were both taking, had, for the moment, put their conversation on pause. However, Blake, being the great talker he is, knew exactly what to say to put Stacey at ease. His mamma, as well as the many older women he came across, had given him a fine lesson in the art of being a "gentleman". "Well, Stacey, he began, I'm sure this is something you don't normally do – allow a stranger to take you to a basketball game," he said with his Cheshire cat smile. She smiled back, and still thinking she was crazy, replied, "You're exactly right. I've never done anything like this." Blake, initially, was a man on a mission and knew how to play the game. He knew he would have to be different from the other men whom she had dated. She would never imagine that he would be totally different from anyone she had ever met.

Blake grew up in a place called Barry Farms, which is located in one of the worst parts of southeast, DC. He was an All-American in three sports in high school, basketball, football, and tennis. He had scholarships from numerous schools throughout the country in all three sports; however, basketball was his number one passion. In his prime, Blake was like

Michael Jordan on most nights. In football and tennis, he was really good, but in basketball, there were not many players who could deal with his game. Blake averaged 29.0 points a game in his senior year of high school and accepted a full scholarship to the University of Florida, mainly because of the weather; but the beautiful women of South Florida were the real selling point. From childhood, women were attracted to Blake as a fat kid is attracted to cake.

Blake had watched his uncle and cousins -who were all big time drug dealers throughout the Washington, DC area- deal with so many beautiful women that he was totally comfortable being in the company of lovely females. Blake's uncle Preach gave him this advice as a youngster: "Find the prettiest girl in the room and get her; then all the women in the room will want you." Most guys had to work really hard to get a woman to notice them, more or less, go out with them, but with Blake, all he had to do was be in the room. He was like a magnet to every gorgeous woman in the place. Blake went through women like a baby Wilt Chamberlain. (For those of you who don't remember, Wilt was linked to 3,000 women during his 'heyday'). However, everything changed in Blake's freshman year when he met Brandi.

During Blake's first month on campus, girls were flocking to him just as they did in high school. The girls would hang around the dorm and practice gym for the basketball team; hoping they would be noticed and would one day turn into a date.

One day while walking to the dorm from basketball practice, Blake noticed this beautiful young lady sitting on the park bench reading a text book. Normally, women would notice the players as they leave the gym, but this young lady could hear them talking but never raised her head to see who was walking in her direction. Blake, being the number one womanizer of the east coast, was dying to get some attention from this student, with the hopes of a new victim. When Blake realized she was not acknowledging his presence, he purposely started talking louder, but it didn't work.

He was now more determined to find out who this young lady was. She paid him no attention and this bothered Blake. He asked a few of his teammates who she was, but no one knew. Normally, Blake would have stepped to her and put the smooth moves on her, but, there was something different about this young lady. Blake stared at her without saying a word; actually, for the first time in his life, he was nervous and afraid – wow! Not Blake.

As the train pulled up to the Rockville station, Blake and Stacey got off and headed upstairs to the street where Blake's friend Kenny was waiting to give him a ride to the games. Blake and Stacey walked towards the car, Kenny got out of the driver's seat to see who was with Blake. "Stacey, this is Kenny, Kenny, Stacey." "Hello Kenny," said Stacey with the soft sexy voice of hers. "Hello sweetheart," Kenny responded. Blake got in the back seat and allowed Stacey to sit up front with Kenny. "Blake, where did you ever find this gorgeous young lady sitting here?" "We just met on the train and she begged to follow me to the game," Blake said jokingly. "That's not true," said Stacey, "I was on my way to the mall; we started conversing on the train when he asked me to come see him play and I said okay." "Damn…baby girl, you just hang out with strangers you meet on the Metro?" "Come on Kenny, you know she could not resist the boyish charm I possess once I started talking to her," said Blake. "Yea right," said Kenny. "Stacey, be very careful with this brother here, he's my main man, apple scrapple, but don't let him feed you a bunch of bull shit and have you spinning in the wind," said Kenny. "What does that mean?" asked Stacey. Kenny could see Blake giving him the 'shut the fuck up' look through the rear view mirror. "Stacey, I'm just kidding, Blake is a good dude, you're in good hands," said Kenny. "Are you sure Kenny?" asked Stacey. "I've known Blake for 15 years now, he's probably my best friend, a real stand up dude," said Kenny. "Okay Kenny, if anything bad happens to me I'm going to blame you," said Stacey. "I got your back baby girl," said Kenny.

On their arrival at the gym, Stacey took a seat in the bleachers while Kenny and Blake headed to the court for the game. Blake's team won 78 to 55. Kenny scored 27 points and Blake 25. Stacey was very impressed with Blake's athleticism and loved the way he looked in his uniform - especially the shorts. Stacey was trying so hard to see the package in his shorts that she could hardly focus on how talented Blake was on the court. After the game, Kenny drove Stacey and Blake downtown Washington, DC for a celebratory drink. They went to a sports bar inside the Grant Hyatt, called the 'Grand Slam'. Kenny and Blake really enjoyed the atmosphere of this establishment; they always watched the "March Madness" basketball games at this location.

While they were having food and drinks, Stacey noticed Kenny admiring a gorgeous looking young lady sitting alone across the room; and wondered why he didn't go over to say something. She whispered to Blake, "Why doesn't Kenny go over and say something to the young lady?" "Kenny is a little shy when it comes to approaching women, as most men are," said Blake. "What?" asked Stacey. On that note, Blake went over to the young lady across the room and asked whether she could join them for a drink or two. Within two seconds, Blake and the woman came to the table where Stacey and Kenny were sitting. "Stacey and Kenny, this is Wanda, Wanda, this is Stacey and Kenny" said Blake. "Hello." "Hello," everyone said at the same time. Wanda said she came down here to watch the game and get out of the house for a few hours said Blake. There was suddenly an awkward silence for a couple seconds because both Blake and Stacey were waiting for Kenny to start a conversation with Wanda, but he just sat there and stared at her without saying a word. However, Blake being Blake, said "So Wanda, why are you in a sports bar on a Sunday night all by yourself, where is your man?" "I don't have a man at this point in my life," said Wanda. "What? ... A pretty girl like you without a man in Washington, DC is unheard of." "Stop playing," said Blake. "Not playing, the brothers I've run across in the city are full of shit and play too many games for me to waste my time," said Wanda. "Well Wanda, tonight is your lucky night" said Blake. "How so?" asked Wanda. "My best friend Kenny is as good as they come, God has blessed you to be in the right place at the right time to meet the right person for you," said Blake. "Oh really?" Wanda remarked. "Kenny, handle this, Stacey and I will be right back," said Blake.

Blake took Stacey for a walk in the hotel. This was with a view to giving Kenny a chance to talk with Wanda without feeling apprehensive by the thought of having others listening. For years, Blake had coached Kenny on the art of easily getting a woman. He was sure to make him understand which ploy to be utilized when a female presents herself before him.

"How did you become so smooth with women?" asked Stacey. "My cousins and uncles taught me at a very young age that most women wanted a confident, respectful man who smells good to approach them and the rest would be easy," said Blake. At that moment, Stacey pushed Blake against the wall and kissed him like he has never been kissed before. After that kiss, Blake said, "Check please!" The kiss was so good he forgot he wasn't in the bar to ask for a check, and Stacey did not hesitate to remind him of their location. Now, all types of thoughts were going through their minds. Not only was the kiss good to Blake; Stacey too was thinking that that was the best kiss she's ever had in her life.

Blake and Stacey returned to the bar and saw Kenny and Wanda having a good time laughing as if they had known each other for years. It turned out; Wanda was from South Carolina, which was coincidentally so was Kenny. Kenny loved talking about how great things were down south compared to the DC area. Blake was very happy to see that Kenny had scored with Wanda; however, Stacey was amazed that Kenny was able to pull it off. While Stacey and Blake were walking and talking in the hotel, Stacey told Blake that she thought Kenny would totally strike out with Wanda. Blake's response was that Kenny had all the tools in his arsenal to get the young lady. Stacey really didn't know what that meant and decided to let it alone and be happy for Kenny.

After a few hours of dining, everyone decided it was time to leave. Blake and Stacey went back to the metro and Kenny and Wanda went to their cars. Blake told Kenny he would catch up with him after work, the day following. While walking to the metro, Blake asked Stacey if she were willing to go to his place for the remainder of the evening. He promised to take her home in the morning in time for work in the event her response was in the affirmative. She subsequently said it wouldn't be a problem.

By this time, those three Long Island ice teas had taken their toll on her decision making. Not to mention that she found Blake incredibly sexy and wanted to make love to him so badly. Stacey seemingly thought to herself that a man who could kiss the way Blake did must be able to make love to her as if there were no tomorrow. Stacey was ecstatic about fulfilling her curiosity.

Blake drove a 528 BMW and lived in a two-bedroom apartment in the better part of Southeast, Washington, DC. His apartment was a typical upscale bachelor pad with all the trimmings. Everything in his apartment was black and red (black leather furniture and red carpet throughout) and was well kept. Blake was also an excellent cook, a skill he picked up from his dad who did 90% of all the cooking when he was growing up. A holder of a degree in Finance, he worked for Georgetown University as the Financial Analyst and at 32 years old, was one of the youngest Directors there.

As Stacey entered Blake's apartment, she noticed how nicely arrayed everything was. The ambience was inviting and relaxing.

After walking through the door, Stacey immediately took off her shoes and went on a self-tour on Blake's invitation. She continued her tour while Blake grabbed champagne from the refrigerator. Blake got the champagne and two glasses and returned to the living room; but Stacey was nowhere to be seen. "Stacey! Where are you?" he called, but there was no answer. Blake checked the bathroom, still there was no Stacey. Blake checked the spare bedroom, there was no Stacey. To Blake's surprise, Stacey was lying on the bed in his bedroom as naked as the day she left her mother's womb. "Oh my goodness!" shouted a startled Blake. "Thank you Jesus!" Blake said to himself as he stood there admiring Stacey's body.

He was anticipating the next move, when suddenly; he felt a tug, as Stacey pulled him closer with all her might. She then removed his belt and started unbuttoning his pants. Once his pants were unbuttoned they fell to the floor. Stacey discovered Blake was wearing boxers and could see from the print that she had gotten lucky with this package. She immediately pulled down the boxers to ensure the package was just the way she thought it would be. You guessed it! The package was exactly what Stacey envisioned. OMG!! Stacey thought to herself. She began to caress his penis with her hands and while doing so; his penis got more erect by the second. Stacey, was now staring up at Blake as to say, "You're about to be served really well." She began sucking his dick like she had cancer and the cure was inside Blake's dick. Blake enjoying every moment of it, stopped her after a few minutes and pushed her back on the bed and penetrated her. He began thrusting inside Stacey's pussy with paced movements, all Stacey could think was, "I've never had a man fuck me this slow and powerful and it feels so damn good." Stacey climaxed within the first two minutes after Blake began.

Blake saw that Stacey's orgasm took her breath away; and he being the ultimate gentleman, asked if she needed a minute to regroup. Stacey was breathing so hard from that orgasm she could barely say yes. Blake lay next to her massaging her back while she caught her breath. No sooner had Stacey got a hold of herself, Blake stretched his arms around her and pinched her nipples. This sent Stacey further into an orgasmic mode. Stacey turned her head to the side to meet Blake's tongue. They kissed again as Blake's left hand reached down between her thighs and began to finger her pussy. Stacey grabbed the back of his neck so as to get more of his tongue closer into her mouth as she grinded her pussy onto his fingers. Within one minute, Stacey achieved another orgasm; this time screaming as if there were no tomorrow. Once again, Blake gave her some time to regroup; then with sarcasm asked, "Can you handle this? I don't want you to die on me." "I'm good; you're just hitting all the right spots so far," Stacey replied.

Blake got up and poured two glasses of champagne he had brought into the room. Stacey was so happy he did, because her mouth was completely dry from the orgasms. "Oh my God! This taste so good," Stacey exclaimed. "Do you drink Moet on a regular basis?" asked Stacey. "Baby girl, this is all I prefer to drink; especially with someone as lovely as you; you deserve the best" replied Blake. Those words from Blake made her melt like butter. She immediately started sucking his dick again. After a few seconds, Blake stopped her and instructed her to turn around. Blake began kissing the back of her neck and continued kissing down her back, while fingering her with his right hand. Stacey again started moaning. Blake then slipped his penis into her pussy from behind. After a few moments, Blake grabbed Stacey around her waist and pulled her towards him until he was no longer on the bed. Blake was now standing up while Stacey was bent over. Blake slid a pillow under Stacey to make her more penetrable. Blake continued fucking Stacey with slow but powerful thrusts which he realized by now was driving her absolutely crazy. After about five minutes, Stacey's moaning got more intense and within thirty seconds she was screaming atop her voice from yet another orgasm. "I'm 'cumming'! I'm 'cumming'! I'm 'cumming'! OMG! OMG!"

Blake thought to himself, "I was absent from church this morning, but it seem as if Stacey is giving me the sermon I missed." Most assuredly, this thought called for an Amen! Meanwhile, Stacey, lying on the bed and obviously breathless, was thinking to herself, "What the hell is going on; my body has never reacted this way, what is this brother doing to me?" Note to self - "Okay, I will cum no more, as this dude is driving me mentally and physically crazy! Get your act together girl…you need not cum again! I had orgasms three times and this dude has not even broken a sweat." On the other side of the bed, Blake was staring into space drinking more Moet and looking as though he was taking a stroll through the park on a Sunday morning. Blake's exterior was cool and calm; he carried himself like nothing rattled him.

Blake then asked Stacey if she would like to watch a movie. Stacey was now thinking "Who is this brother, he doesn't care if he 'cums'?" Stacey snapping back to reality responded "Sure, a movie would be great." Blake got out of bed and went to the living room to select a DVD; he came back with "Love Jones" then placed the DVD into its slot on the player and went to the kitchen to get snacks for two. Blake came back with peeled spicy shrimp, chips and another bottle of Moet. Stacey, was staring at him in amazement, no brother in her life had ever treated her as he did – neither in nor out of bed. She was now feeling great about the choice she made to take the chance while on the Metro.

As they watched the movie, enjoying the shrimp and chips, many thoughts started going through Stacey's mind. "How can a fine ass man being so thoughtful not have a girlfriend, significant other or something?" She so badly wanted to ask those questions, but, she didn't want to mess up the good vibe they had going. Everything was going too good to throw serious conversation in the mix at the moment.

Stacey could tell Blake was the type of man who enjoyed life to the fullest. He was so easy to talk to and he always provided the perfect answer for any given matter they talked about. Stacey started having the typical female thought, "Is he the one?"

As they lay in bed watching the movie, Blake started asking Stacey questions about her childhood, job and things that interested her. It turned out Stacey also grew up in the DC area, but attended high school in Maryland. After completing high school, she went to Penn State University on a track scholarship; which explained why her body was so amazing. She told Blake that she ran the 100 and 200m in high school and college and still had the body to prove it. Stacey worked for the Federal Government as a Financial Analyst as she majored in Finance and Economics. She also graduated Magna Cum Laude, which meant she is a smart and hard worker. Blake was totally impressed with everything about Stacey and was now wondering why Stacey didn't have a boyfriend, significant other or someone in her life. He thought about asking but decided against it. Blake was totally used to meeting ladies like Stacey on a daily basis. For Blake, this was 'just another day at the office'. He recalled that Stacey had mentioned that she found it very difficult to meet a man on her level in DC. She wished they could bring something more to the table than 'dick'. That last comment had Blake laughing so hard because he had heard that so many times from almost every woman he met. The ratio for men to women in the DC area had been 10:1 for the past 40 years; and if a good man were factored, with a good job, excellent credit and not gay, the numbers would be 100:1. Fortunately Blake fell in the latter category and he was cognizant of it.

Blake had a rare confidence about himself without being arrogant. He was a very humble person due to his upbringing by his parents. They kept Blake well-grounded and instilled the proper values in life that made him the ideal catch for the right woman. However, there was one side of Blake that was not so wonderful - his loyalty to his drug dealing cousins and uncles. There were times that Blake would help them make some moves (for a major fee of course) that could cost him his life and career. This activity didn't happen often but indeed took place from time to time. Blake was extremely smart and well respected on both sides of the track. As a result, there were certain major drug suppliers who would not deal with Blake's family, they would only make the transaction through Blake, and for his services his family paid him 10 percent of the amount that was spent to acquire the product. A typical transaction would be between Fifty and one hundred thousand dollars. With this, Blake was making anywhere from five to ten thousand dollars per transaction. On average, Blake was supplementing his income by sixty to one hundred thousand dollars per year. This was in surplus of his regular one hundred and thirty thousand dollar salary at Georgetown University. Blake was clearing close to two Hundred, fifty thousand a year. This, coupled with the fact that he was single, educated, intelligent, nice on the eyes, great in bed, extremely kind and a complete gentleman made him 'Mr. Right' to every woman he met.

Blake realized that his way with women was both a blessing and a curse. Blake knew that he must always deal with a very strong woman or he would be setting himself up for drama or even a stalker. It had happened too many times; he's therefore aware of the potential risk with being with a woman who is not self-confident.

It was now about half way through the movie - Blake who was spooning with Stacey as they watched the movie, started kissing her on the back of her neck. Stacey immediately got on top of him, grabbed his dick and stuck it in her pussy. Stacey began riding Blake as a cowboy would his favorite horse. During the action, Stacey got up and made a 360 degree turn - now riding with her back facing Blake. Unlike Blake being on top, Stacey is moving really fast, Blake had to tell her to slow down. The funny part was, within a minute of him telling her to slow down, Stacey started another orgasm.

Stacey needed a moment to catch her breath as Blake lay in admiration for being able to please her so many times. As Stacey sat atop Blake, she confessed "I've never had this many orgasms in my life before." "Who are you?" she asked. Blake had a little smile on his face and said "The reason you are 'cumming' so much is because you're taking your time. I'm pretty sure you're used to having sex as fast as a rabbit. Sex should always be a slow but powerful process. "You must be right, because my body is doing things it has never done before" said Stacey. "I am curious about something, why haven't you cum yet?" Stacey asked. "I've been taught to totally please a woman before I get mine. A man will always 'cum', however, some women struggle with this issue, especially those who really don't know their bodies, so I like to figure out who I'm dealing with and please her accordingly," replied Blake. Those words seemed to take Stacey's feelings for Blake to an all-time high. "Wow, I've never heard another man articulate as well as you do. You seem to always know what to do and what to say in any given situation, that is such a turn-on," said Stacey. After that statement, Blake hoisted Stacey from his dick and left the room. Stacey was a little puzzled, thinking she had said something wrong. After a few seconds, Blake returned with an armless chair from his dining room table. He sat in the chair and then asked Stacey to join him. Stacey, now looking happy about what would come next, gladly joined Blake. He positioned her on his dick while sitting in the chair, this turned out to be the most exciting position for both Stacey and Blake. They both started fucking each other like the world would truly end the moment they finished. For the first time today, Stacey was hearing Blake moan and the sound drove her crazy. After about ten minutes or so, Blake started staring into Stacey's eyes with the most intense look she had ever seen from a man, then suddenly, they both started 'cumming' and screaming, "Oh Shit! Oh Shit! Oh Shit!" screamed Blake, "OMG! OMG! OMG! OMG!" screamed Stacey. They both were totally out of breath and couldn't talk to each other. When they caught their breath, they both started laughing and talking about how great it was. At this point, Stacey seemed convinced that Blake was the man she had been seeking as a soul mate and future husband; funny how great sex can trigger these thoughts in a woman. For most men, having great sex was 'just another day at the office'. To be clear, most men need to be hit with a bolt of lightning before those feelings surfaced, if the lighting didn't come, it would be just sex.

After that wonderful night of passion, Stacey and Blake hooked up a few more times before Stacey started pressing Blake for them to have a committed relationship. Blake explained to Stacey that at this point of his life, he was emotionally unavailable. Stacey felt that Blake wanted to keep his options open for being with other women. As a result, she stopped calling him and moved on with her life. Blake's escapade with most women would usually end in this manner. So Blake dropped Stacey like people drop bad habits and started reflecting on his life prior to meeting Stacey.

CHAPTER 2

A Special Spot

Blake was having a hard time concentrating in practice and more-so in the classroom because of the young lady he saw a month ago. He was dying to know who this young lady was – her not paying attention to him was still a bother. Blake started asking his friends who were mostly jocks, but no one seemed to know the particular girl.

One day, Blake ran into her at the local Subway, sandwich shop which was a block away from campus. As Blake walked in to get a sandwich after practice, he noticed her in the corner of the shop eating a sub sandwich and reading one of her text books. Blake remembered the first time he saw her she was reading a book. He figured she was a very smart student. Blake was right, Brandi was a straight 'A' student who had a four year full academic scholarship. She was raised in Richmond, VA, but most of her family lived in the Washington, DC area. Her dad had his own dental practice and her mom was a nurse at the Washington Hospital Center. Brandi attended Mary Washington High School, which was an all-girl private school. Brandi was not only smart, she played volleyball, softball and ran track for her high school. She was an All- American volleyball player but loved softball and running track. Brandi enjoyed team sports because of the camaraderie she had with her teammates.

Brandi received many scholarship offers for volleyball all across the country but her goal in life was to become a Software Engineer. At a very young age, Brandi was a computer genius in most people eyes. By the time she turned 13 years old; Brandi took her hard drive completely apart and rebuilt it with no problem. Everyone said she would be the next Bill Gates. Brandi stood 5 feet 8 inches and looked like Gabrielle Union's twin sister. Men were completely mesmerized when they saw her. When she spoke, her stock went through the roof. She was smart, pretty, and sexy, with a personality that blew most people away, even women. Brandi had the most humbling spirit one could imagine. Most women who looked like her were usually self-centered and arrogant. Not Brandi, she made everyone around her feel as though they were the most important person in the room. Brandi's parents gave her a spirit base that was totally centered on God. She would put God first in anything she did. Brandi was the type of woman that all men were looking for as a mate for life.

Blake knew this was the opportune time to meet Brandi. He ordered food and walked over to Brandi who had her head buried in her text book. "Excuse me, would you mind if I sat with you?" he asked. She instantly remembered him as the jock that came out of the gym a few weeks ago, trying to get her attention by talking loudly. "There are plenty empty seats in the shop, if you don't mind, can you sit somewhere else? I really need to study. Thank you," replied Brandi. "No problem" said Blake, but he was really pissed. Blake sat at another table facing Brandi and pretty much stared at her for the next 45 minutes until Brandi left. "Damn, this girl won't give me the time of day, what the fuck is going on?" Blake asked himself. He sat there for another 15 minutes trying to come up with a plan for getting Brandi to talk with him. This encounter was mentally draining for Blake; he never had to work at getting a girl to talk to him. Brandi had Blake losing sleep over the situation. He started having dreams of Brandi – these dreams would wake him up at odd times during the night. Blake tried to let it go, but every time he would see Brandi in the yard, his mind would start racing and crazy feelings would overtake him.

PREACH

One day, after seeing Brandi walking across the campus, Blake thought to himself, "I'm in love with a stranger." Blake knew he needed to get a grip of the situation but he didn't know what to do. This was completely unfamiliar territory for Blake, so he decided to call his uncle Preach and get advice on how to handle what he considered a weird situation.

"Yo Preach, what's up dude?" asked Blake "Hey nephew, what's shaking down there in Florida?" said Preach. "I got a situation I need to run by you," said Blake. "Oh yea, do I need to strap up and come down there to handle something?" asked Preach. "Nah, nothing like that, it's a female." "What? Nigger you got more butt than an ashtray, so what problem could you have with a female? Is somebody pregnant? Did you catch something?" "No, nothing close to anything you mentioned," said Blake. "Then, what else could it be?" asked Preach. "I really don't know how to say this," said Blake. "Mother Fucker, for your black ass to call me from Florida, something serious is up, what isit?" asked an annoyed Preach. "Don't laugh," said Blake. "Boy, stop playing with me and just say it," said Preach. "Okay, it's this girl I saw a couple weeks ago after basketball practice. Preach, she is all that and a bag a chips. The problem is the girl will neither look at nor speak to me. I tried twice now to get her to talk to me but to no avail – nothing came of it Preach. Actually, the last time I tried, she totally shut me down," said Blake. "Let me get this straight, you call me from Florida, getting my blood pressure up because you can't get some pussy from one girl," said Preach." "Preach, she is the one; she is not the typical girl I deal with. Yes, I've had some bad chicks but this one crushes them all, she has a special spot," said Blake. "Damn…she like that?" asked Preach. "Yes," I wouldn't have called you had she not been like that. Think about it, how many times have you seen me not being able to get any girl I wanted?" asked Blake. "Maybe that's the problem, you've never had to work at it like most of us, your ass is spoiled, and now sounds like you have a real challenge on your hands," said Preach. "Why you think I'm calling you" said Blake. "What's her name?" asked Preach. "I don't know," said Blake. "Boy, you going crazy over some pussy and don't even know her name," said Preach. "Yep," said Blake. "Damn, she has to be all that and more for Mr. Blake Dawson to go through all this trouble for a woman whose name he doesn't even know," said Preach. "She is," said Blake. "Tell you what, do your homework on this one -meaning, find out her name, where she is from, if she comes from money and even if she has mother and father. "Find out as much as you can and call me back with the information and I will have a sure fire, slam dunk plan to get her, trust me," said Preach. "I'm on it," said Blake. "Before you go, make sure you do not try to talk to her or even be around her until I get the information and give you the plan," said Preach. "I got you," said Blake.

Over the next week, Blake started gathering information as his uncle instructed. He followed her to her dorm one day and after she walked past the front desk attendant and got on the elevator, Blake went to the front desk and told the attendant that the girl who just got on the elevator dropped a $20 bill from her back pocket and he wanted to return it. The attendant asked Blake to give her the $20 and she would make sure it was returned. Blake refused and the attendant called her on the loud speaker for the building "Brandi Green, you're needed at the front desk, Brandi Green; you're needed at the front desk." After hearing her name, Blake gave the attendant the $20 dollar bill and said "You know what? I trust that you will give it to her." He rolled out before Brandi arrived.

Armed with the newly acquired information, Blake immediately went to his dorm to get on his laptop. "Brandi…such a beautiful name for a beautiful person," Blake thought to himself. Blake started his research and found out where she was from, who her parents were, what her parents did for a living, and everything that Brandi was involved with in high school. He was very delighted to find out she was into sports and dedicated to her school work. He also learned that Brandi had a full scholarship just like he had; the only difference was his scholarship was based on athletics. Blake now more than ever thought there was a strong connection between the two and must be explored.

Blake continuing the instructions from his uncle Preach called and provided him the information researched. Preach told Blake to give him a few days and he would get back to him with a game plan to take her down. After three days, Blake got a call from Preach, "Baby boy, how is it hanging?" said Preach. "What's up uncle Preach?" asked Blake. "Well, I have good news and bad news. Which do you want first?" asked Preach. "Give me the bad news first" said Blake. "Son, she is out of your league, move on and stop thinking about her, Risk vs. Reward" said Preach. "Then what's the good news?" asked Blake. "The good news is, you found out right away so you don't have to waste any more time thinking about this girl. You just continue knocking down four to five girls a week, like I know you've been. Blake, remember this wisdom - you can't have every girl you want, and there will always be that one that a man wants, but will never get. Risk vs. Reward. You just happened to find that one person early in life which is a good thing, trust me," said Preach.

From the time he was a child, uncle Preach always gave Blake the best advice possible and was on point with everything he said. Blake trusted uncle Preach 1000% when it came to getting a female. He had watched his uncle worked the ladies for many years which is how he learned the craft. "Okay Preach, I'm done with that. In fact, I saw this cutie leaving practice today and I think I will hook up with her tonight," said Blake. "That's my apple scrapple - for not getting Ms. Brandi you should have a three-some tonight, it will make you forget about Brandi even quicker," said Preach. "Will do sir," said Blake. Even though Blake told his uncle that he would follow his advice, he had no intentions on doing a three-some. Blake was totally focused on Brandi and could not and would not let it go as there was a special spot.

For the next several years at the University of Florida, Blake became a different person. He no longer had the desire to be with different women everyday as in the past. Seeing Brandi somehow changed him as a person. Blake started to realize that there was much more to life than knocking down beautiful women night after night, even though he really and truly enjoyed those conquests. Brandi's impact on Blake was enormous; Blake was now more serious about his studies. It was as if he was determined to be as smart as she was. Blake even severed ties with his starting five. (Girls that he would have sex with Monday-Friday).

Blake would only get with a girl for sex when he really needed. (It's a man thing – and only a man would understand).

For the next three years, Blake focused on his academics. Basketball, which had always been number one in his life, took a backseat to the new Blake Dawson, just imagine - all this was credited to a girl who wouldn't even talk to him.

As the years went by, it didn't matter, Brandi was branded into Blake's soul forever. How often does something like this happen to a young man from the ghetto? One day towards the end of the semester during Blake's junior year, he was sitting on the bench where he first saw Brandi. He was studying for his final exams when a soft angelic voice said, "What are you doing sitting in my spot?" Blake, who had his head buried in his book looked up; and to his surprise it was Brandi who had made the comment. Blake - totally stunned that after three years and without coercion the girl of his dreams spoke to him. "Wow! You spoke to me," said Blake. "What do you mean?" asked Brandi. "Girl, I've been trying to get your attention for three years and you finally spoke to me today," Blake replied. "Why were you trying to get my attention Blake Dawson?" asked Brandi. "You know my name?" said Blake. "I know many things about you which is the reason I purposely stayed away" said Brandi. Blake was so caught up in the fact that Brandi spoke to him, he didn't even notice that Brandi was wearing a graduation cap and gown. "I graduated from the School of Engineering just a few minutes ago and wanted to come to my special spot on campus and reminisce about the hard work I put in to get me to this point with my degree. I loved studying on this bench, for some strange reason, this spot was a sense of peace for me and it made me feel that whatever I studied would be retained because I did it here. I know this all probably sounds crazy to you, but, I have a special spiritual connection to this bench – God is here," said Brandi. Blake was totally blown away by Brandi's words, her faith and her overall total being. "You may not believe this, but I believe and I feel the same way about this location," said Blake. "I saw you trying to get my attention like three years ago, but, I felt like you were being the typical man trying to get some ass, and I wasn't having it," said Brandi. Blake, the smoothest talking brother on the planet was stuck; he truly didn't know what to say to Brandi. "Can you sit down and chat for a moment?" asked Blake. "That's why I came to this bench; I just didn't think anyone would be here this early in the day," said Brandi.

To Blake's delight, Brandi took a seat on the bench and they talked for hours. Their conversation was so good, 4 hours had gone by and it felt like 20 minutes. Neither of them wanted to end the conversation.

RISK vs. REWARD

Brandi explained to Blake why she wouldn't give him the time of day for the past three years. She told him that all the girls in her dorm were talking about this brother from Washington, DC who was all that, in the sheets and out. She went on to say that it would not have been so bad, but it seemed like too many women had the same story which suggested that he was on campus banging them all. On that note, she committed to herself that it would never happen to her. Brandi continued by saying that many women including her, thought Blake was quite handsome and had a pretty good basketball game. "Really?" asked Blake. "I didn't realize you were a year ahead of me. When I first saw you, I thought you were a freshman like me," said Blake. "I was a freshman with you; however, I finished my four year degree in three years with the help of this Godly bench we're sitting on," said Brandi. "You are truly remarkable," said Blake. "I give all the glory to God," said Brandi. "I do have one confession," said Brandi. "What's that?" asked Blake. "After talking to you today, I really wish I would have talked with you sooner. You seem to be so cool. My first perception of you was not good, my bad," said Brandi." "No problem, to be honest your perception was not that far off during my freshman year." They both laughed and gave each other a high five. However, at that moment, like a bolt of lightning, Brandi was struck by the Blake charm. She was so excited about being with him she could barely contain herself. Luckily for her, Blake didn't realize what had just taken place. For whatever reason, Brandi wanted to kiss him so badly and because of these feelings, Blake could sense that something was wrong; he just didn't know what was going on in Brandi's mind.

Brandi was a virgin and never really had many sexual feeling. She didn't allow her mind to wander in that direction, but today was truly a special day; her mind was lost heading that direction. Brandi could feel herself getting wet. She was now becoming extremely nervous around Blake. "What do I do? What do I do?" she kept asking herself.

"Would it be okay if I gave you a congratulatory hug for your accomplishment today?" asked Blake. "I guess that would be okay," said Brandi. Blake stood, and then grabbed Brandi by her hand to help her up. They both embraced like Michelle and Barack when he was announced President of the United States. Blake could tell that Brandi was enjoying the hug so he didn't let go. Brandi was on cloud nine; her mind had completely left her body. Brandi was floating on the clouds and could not be found. After almost a minute into her float, Brandi's eyes connected with Blake's and locked as if their minds were speaking to each other. Blake and Brandi leaned forward and began kissing. Blake was kissing Brandi so passionately, that her juices between her legs increased. They kissed for at least a minute with so much fire, passion and desire for each other.

After the kiss, Brandi stared at Blake and never said a word. Blake just stared back at Brandi; somehow, it was if they both knew what just happened was magic. Without saying a word, Blake grabbed Brandi by her hand and they started walking towards her dorm. When they reached the building, Blake kissed Brandi again, this time; it was short and sweet. He told her that he had to go finish studying for his finals so that he could be just like her. Blake turned and walked away with Brandi standing there looking at him, thinking "Are you seriously going to leave me here horny as hell and wanting you like I've never wanted anyone in my life?" The truth is, during their time sitting on the bench Blake realized that the torch he had been carrying for Brandi was about to burn out because Brandi was leaving both him and school. The thought of possibly never seeing her again became overwhelming.

He heard his uncle's words ringing in his head, "let that go and move on"– an advice he didn't take and now it was about to cost him emotionally. Blake realized during the walk to the dorm that he finally could have Brandi, but, she was the first and only girl he did not want to have a fling with, Brandi was for keeps. From Blake's standpoint, she was the one for him, and he had reserved a special spot in his heart for her, so he knew this would hurt for a while.

Brandi's influence on Blake caused him to change a great deal; he still would have flings with women, but not as often as before, and each time he did, it was no longer fun and he knew it. Blake, because of the recent attention to his studies improved his academic standing – a GPA which stood at 2.7 before Brandi had moved up to 3.6.

Brandi was now gone from his life and Blake had to mentally move – this wasn't as easy as he thought it would have been. He found himself comparing Brandi with every woman he met and unfortunately, no one measured up. Somewhere deep in Blake's heart, he knew one day he would see her again and she would be his for keeps. So for now; all Blake had was a day of memories and the bench that made him felt spiritually close to her.

This bench became Blake's refuge, when he was sad, when he had problems, and when he was happy about something, he would go to the bench. Some students on campus thought he was a little weird because they would quite often find him talking to himself while sitting studying and looking into space. Blake thought to himself, "Funny how a woman you don't know can change your entire outlook on life;" which was exactly what Brandi did to Blake.

CHAPTER 3

Connections

A few months later, Blake graduated with a degree in Finance and landed a job at Price Waterhouse Coopers (PWC). He was junior Auditor and generally handled non-profit organizations. His area of expertise was internal controls for revenue and grants. Blake traveled quite a bit during his first three years with the firm and in his third year became the lead auditor for grant projects.

Blake was happy with the work he was doing but hated the travel schedule which had him living from a suitcase most of the year. Blake would spend up to three months out of town and be home for one week and at the end of that week, he would be headed to another client in another state. Living in hotels and eating hotel food got old quickly for Blake. As a result, he told a couple of friends to be on the lookout for potential job opportunities within his field.

Within two months, one of his buddies contacted him about an opening at Georgetown University. "Blake, what's up dude?" said Tim. "Hey Tim, what's going on?" said Blake. "John told me you were job hunting and we have a Financial Analyst position that became available two days ago. I need you to email your résumé to me so I can hand deliver it to the hiring manager; she is a very good friend of mine." "Word?" asked Blake. "Yes, I got you. Hopefully, I can at least get you an interview but the onus would be on you to take it home from there," said Tim. "I can do that," said Blake. Two weeks later, Blake was contacted by the Hiring Manager, Gina Pearson, who was also the Assistant Treasurer. She had sent him an email enquiring of his availability for the coming Monday. Blake responded, advising he was leaving for an audit in Texas on Sunday and would not return to the DC area for two months. Mrs. Pearson asked if he could see her the Friday before his trip. Blake agreed and they scheduled the interview for Friday at 10:00 am at her office.

Blake arrived at Mrs. Pearson's office Friday at 9:30 am. Mrs. Pearson was notified by her Administrative Assistant that Mr. Dawson was in the lobby for his interview. About 9:50 am, Mrs. Pearson invited him to her office. Mrs. Pearson was a woman in her late fifties; she stood about 5 feet 3 inches tall and had a very serious disposition. During the interview, Mrs. Pearson was very interested in Blake's sports achievements. It turned out; she related sports with office in the areas of teamwork and working under pressure. She was extremely pleased to hear that Blake was a big time scorer, as it suggested he would be able to make decisions on matters of a highly pressured nature. At the end of the interview Mrs. Pearson told Blake that she had one last question for him - "If your team were losing by one point with three seconds to go, are you the person that makes the assist or the person who takes the shot? Without hesitation, Blake responded, "I take the shot every time." "You're hired!" said Mrs. Pearson. "Seriously?" asked Blake. "As long as your background check is good and your references are okay, the job is yours," said Mrs. Pearson. Blake left that interview extremely happy and thankful to his friend Tim.

"Tim, I nailed it! Mrs. Pearson and I totally hit it off, she is mad cool," said Blake. "Yes she is," said Tim. "I will leave on Sunday for Texas, so I told her my start date could be the moment I returned," said Blake. "Sounds good," said Tim. On Sunday, Blake flew to Texas for what he considered his last audit. Upon his arrival at the hotel, he sent Mrs. Pearson a thank you email and provided her with his hotel phone number in the event she needed additional information from him while he was away.

Two weeks into his trip, when Blake returned to his room after a day at the office, he received a voice message from Mrs. Pearson stating that his background check and references were found to be satisfactory and that the job was officially his. She asked him for the hotel's fax number with the intent on sending him the offer letter for him to sign and return to her as soon as he could. Blake provided the fax number and received the offer letter. He immediately sent the signed copy back to Mrs. Pearson, which she confirmed receipt and everything was now complete. Blake realized that Mrs. Pearson was very much by the book for all business transactions of the University.

Blake's start date was one week after his assignment ended in Texas. He knew his family and friends would be overjoyed with the news that he would finally be home to stay. Blake spent the next six months glued to Mrs. Pearson as she taught him all the different processes and procedures of cash management. Mrs. Pearson also loved the fact that Blake had an extensive internal control and financial background. She realized that her skillset complimented his skillset and vice versa. Blake was able to pick up the cash management processes very quickly while also implementing internal controls in areas that were lacking oversight. Mrs. Pearson taught Blake how to send domestic and international wires, as well as setting up direct deposit systems, cash management forecasting and actuals vs. budgeted for monthly and daily projections. She trained Blake on investment management and debt covenant regulations and introduced him to her style of supervising employees, which was strict on accountability and performance. Transparency and service delivery were her theme phrase on a daily basis.

The pairing of Mrs. Pearson and Blake was a match made in heaven and they both knew it. They worked very well together and this led to them becoming really good personal friends. Mrs. Pearson knew Blake totally had her back and Blake knew the same. After one year, they could finish each other's sentences. It was weird and great at the same time. For the first time since Blake began his professional career, he was totally happy with his job, the work, the environment and he loved his boss. Not very often can anyone say all of those traits exist at their workplaces. Blake tremendously enjoyed working on the college campus, as working on a college campus meant "eye candy" was everywhere. Blake didn't walk around the campus much, but when he did, he could feel those young girls staring and wishing. However, Blake was too mature to even consider ruining his career for a young piece of ass. He had too many administrative and faculty workers that were admiring him any time he stepped on campus. To Blake's credit, he didn't believe in having relationships with co-workers. That was a strict rule with Blake and he was always in compliance.

One day a student came to his office to complain about a cashier whom he supervised and when this particular student walked in his office, all Blake could think was "OMG, WTF". This young lady was drop dead gorgeous from head to toe and when she spoke she instantly reminded him of Brandi. Her voice was so soft and sexy Blake could barely concentrate on what she was saying to him. As the young lady explained her problem, Blake knew he needed to get his assistant to handle the situation, however, when he called her extension, there was no answer. Blake wanted to get up from his desk to locate her, but, due to the incredible beauty of this young lady, Blake didn't dare stand up or it would be very obvious that he would not be standing alone. His member was already standing at attention (If you know what I mean).

Blake made small talk with the student until the coast was clear to get up and go to his assistant. He found the assistant in the office kitchen having lunch. "Michelle, could you please assist this student in my office, she is having a problem with one of the cashiers and I'm tied up with this report that's due to Mrs.

Pearson in the next thirty minutes," said Blake. The truth was, for the first time in a long time, here was a woman who excited every inch of Blake, which hadn't happen since Brandi. Even though Blake tried to not think about her, something would always happen to remind him of what he considered the woman of his dreams. Now that Blake was out of school and back in DC daily, he spent more time with his cousins and uncle Preach. He really enjoyed being around his uncle Preach more so than his cousins even though his uncle Preach was twenty years older. From Blake's perspective, his cousins had a tendency to get caught up with a lot of drama that came with the drug game and being around them could potentially get Blake into something he would regret for the rest of his life. Now, Preach was one of those smooth 'old school' hustlers. Preach was a very smart dude who always weighed risk against reward. His philosophy was "if you're going to sell drugs, you should make at least $50K a month, anything less than that, you need a job and get out the game." Preach always told Blake that it would be stupid for someone selling drugs and only making $5K to $10K a month, because if we both get caught, the dude making $5K to 10K will get the same amount of jail time I get, but I'm making $100K to $200K a month and living life to the fullest. "Risk vs. Reward!!" Preach said that phrase every day since Blake could remember. It was funny how he would use it in almost every situation that arose. Blake thought back to when he gave him the information about Brandi and he told him to leave it alone and move on "Risk vs. Reward" was what he said and Blake never questioned him to know what he really meant at that time; but in the back of his mind, he knew that one day the answer would be revealed.

One of Blake's favorite cousins was Gary. Gary had been selling drugs since he was 12 years old. He started by selling weed, but, uncle Preach took Gary and some of the other cousins into the fast money world of cocaine. Preach had a talk with the cousins one day and told them they were working hard but not smart. He told them that they were investing too much time and the risk was definitely not worth the reward - Risk vs Reward was just not there. He said, "Why work 12 hours a day and make $500, when you can work 2 hours a day and make $5000." Of course, this concept was very appealing to all the cousins, so before one could blink, all the cousins were selling cocaine that was being supplied to them by Uncle Preach. As usual, uncle Preach was right, the cousins went from making $500 a day to sometimes $5000 a day. And with their increase in cash flow, there was a major increase in partying, shopping and the women.

The quantity and quality of women the cousins started having also changed drastically. On a scale of 1 to 10, the quality went from 5 to 10. All of a sudden, everyone had what is referred to as "dimes" in a man's world. The cousins wouldn't even speak to a female if she weren't at least a size 8, and that's from head to toe. Every time Blake ran into one of his cousins, a female in the range of Lisa Raye was on his arm. Life for Blake also started to change with the decision for everyone to sell cocaine; what use to be a call once a month turned into a call once a week. Blake was much more conservative than his cousins and stashed the cash he was making on the side with a very good friend of his named Michelle. Michelle and Blake grew up together in Barry Farms and had known each other since they were 5 years old. Michelle worked at SunTrust Bank as a Teller Manager, so Blake would always give her the side money to ease into a special account she had setup for him. Michelle knew not to ever deposit more than $10K at any one time because of Internal Revenue Service (IRS) regulations to report those funds. One year, Michelle, notified Blake that he had over $250K in his account; and that he really needed to think about some investment options. Blake was always very low keyed about his extra-curricular activities to earn extra income; especially from his parents and other family members.

Blake was seen as the bright shining star of the family. He was the first and only male cousin in the family that went to college and graduated, and his family was so proud of that accomplishment.

Everything important that happened in the family had to get Blake's approval. The family held strongly to the view that Blake was the smartest person who would and could fix any problem that arose. Whenever anyone had a problem - whether financially, medically, emotionally or otherwise; they would call Blake for guidance. Above all else, Blake loved his family more than life itself, and he made sure they knew it every chance he got.

From time to time, Blake would treat the entire family to lavish trips to Atlantic City, the Bahamas and special outings within the city. He really enjoyed making his family happy and partying of any sort made them happy. Blake's family loved drinking, smoking, dancing and eating great food. There were some really great cooks in the family, so all family gatherings were always so great and included lots of fun. Blake made it a rule never to take a girl to any family gathering, because of what happened the one time he actually took someone to a family function.

During the summer, approximately three years ago, Blake had met this girl called Linda Moore. She was shopping with her mom and little sister when Blake saw her through the window of the Victoria Secret store. Blake actually did a double take when he saw her because she was so nice looking. Blake carefully considered approaching her, however, the fact that she was with her mother made it difficult for him.

RISK vs. REWARD

Blake, being now totally immersed in the machinations of getting any woman he desired was going to figure out a way to get her attention. With this, he rushed over to the Godiva shop and purchased a box of very expensive chocolate. He wrote a note on the back of his business card and had the store clerk tape it to the box. The clerk placed the box in the signature bag of Godiva. Blake was now ready to make his move.

He walked into the Victoria Secret store and approached Linda, her mom and little sister. "Excuse ladies, a gentleman in a gray pinstriped suit asked me to deliver this package to you," said Blake directing his attention to Linda. He handed her the package and walked outside the store. He pretended as if he was waiting on someone as the ladies exited the store. "Excuse me sir, who is the man that gave you this package?" asked Linda. "I don't know the guy, he only asked me if I would be willing to hand you the package and gave me $50 for doing so. He said he had never seen someone as beautiful as you and he wanted to see if he could make you smile," said Blake. "Really?" asked Linda. "He was staring at you and your family while you were in the store," said Blake.

"Wow, the gift is really nice, but the words on the back of his card – Wow they are breath-taking…was he wearing a wedding ring? What did he look like?" asked Linda. "He was a tall dude in a pinstriped suit. I really didn't pay much attention." "Girl, why would he notice those things about another man?" Linda's mom asked. "You're right, but damn, I would love to have seen him," said Linda. "Well, you got his card, so you know he has a job, finds you attractive and has good taste; that should be enough to call him immediately," said the mother. "Oh, I almost forgot, the dude did have on some nice ass crocks, I did notice that," said Blake. "Thanks a lot and sorry for badgering you sir," said Linda. "No problem; just make sure I get an invite to the wedding," said Blake laughing as he walked away.

It was a good thing Blake walked away when he did because Linda called the cell number on the card two minutes later. Blake purposely didn't answer and allowed it to go into voicemail. "Hello, my name is Linda and you gave a guy a bag of candy to give me here at the mall. If you're still in the mall give me a call back right away," said Linda.

Blake didn't return the call until the next day; he knew how to make a woman's desire increase when she wanted something. "Hello, may I speak with Linda?" said Blake. "This is she," said Linda. "I got your message this morning; it's a pleasure to put the voice to the beautiful face I saw yesterday. I hope I wasn't being too forward in sending you the little gift. I was really blown away watching you in the store with your family. Do you like the gift?" "The gift was great, but what you said on the back of your card blew me away," said Linda. "Everything I wrote was true based on what I saw," said Blake. "Wow, that's extremely flattering, you're making me blush early in the morning," said Linda. "Stop playing, you appeared to be too confident to be blushing," said Blake. "You're making me blush even more now," said Linda while laughing.

"So Linda, who are you? Go right ahead and tell me a little more about you," said Blake. "I'm 27, graduated from the University of South Carolina with a degree in Social Work. I'm single, no children yet and I'm still looking for the man of my dreams." "So who are you Mr. Dawson?" "I'm 32, single, I graduated from the University of Florida with a degree in Finance, I have no kids yet and I'm looking to enjoy life to the fullest. As you saw from my business card, I work at Georgetown University." "What do you look like? You've seen me but I haven't seen you yet, and that's not fair" said Linda. "Well, if you're not busy today, my family is having a cookout at 2:00 pm." said Blake. "I'm totally free today, where can I meet you?" "Meet me? Can't I pick you up?" asked Blake. "I would have to know you before you can know where I live," said Linda. "Understood," said Blake. "Can you meet me at the Burger King in Eastover Shopping Center at 2:00 pm?" "Do you know where that is?" asked Blake. "I know where it is.

What kind of car will you be in?" asked Linda. "I drive a silver BMW," said Blake. "What about you?" asked Blake?" "A blue Honda Accord," said Linda. "Cool, see you at 2," said Blake.

Blake arrived at the Burger King location at 1:55 pm, Linda was already there eager to see her mystery man. Blake pulled up right next to Linda but didn't get out the car. Linda was looking at the silver BMW that pulled up next to her waiting for him to get out; Blake purposely just sat there until Linda could take it no more. Linda got out of her car and approached Blake's driver window. Blake's windows were tinted so Linda had no idea she was in for a surprise. Linda tapped on the window and Blake slowly lowered the window and to Linda's surprise, it was the guy who delivered the package. "Oh my God, my mother was right. On the way home she said you might be the guy who gave me the package," said Linda. "Are you disappointed?" asked Blake. "Not at all, my mom and I were talking about how cute you were and too bad you weren't the guy. You really played that part... you bastard," said Linda laughing. "You got me good, all night long I was wondering and praying that you were nice looking."

Blake got out of the car and gave Linda a big hug and kiss on the cheek for being a good sport. Linda was very impressed with Blake's warmth and personality. "I have one more surprise for you before we take off," said Blake. Blake hit the button on his key chain and opened the trunk of his car. He had a bottle of Moet inside a cooler sitting in a pool of ice with two champagne glasses that were perfectly chilled. Blake popped open the bottle, poured two glasses and made a toast. "To a beautiful woman with a great sense of humor, I pray this is the first day of many wonderful days with you." "Wow!! I must admit, you are hitting all the right buttons Mr. Dawson." "Cheers!" They clicked the two glasses together and took a drink. At this point, Linda began looking into Blake's eyes as if to say... are you for real or am I dreaming. Linda was extremely happy she made that call. Linda and Blake stood in the parking lot drinking Moet and talking but before you knew it, one hour had flown by. "You ready to go?" asked Blake. "Yes." Linda responded. Blake opened the passenger door to his car and Linda got in. The cookout was at Blake's parents' house in Fort Washington, MD.

When Blake and Linda arrived, a good number of family members were already there. As they entered the house, everyone was staring at Linda, trying to figure out who she was. Blake is not known for bringing people to family gatherings, so this was a rare occasion for everyone - especially Blake. As Blake and Linda made their way to the kitchen, they saw Blake's mom frying chicken. "Hey Ma!" said Blake. "My son, so good to see you," "Who is this beautiful lady with you?" "Ma, this is Linda, Linda this is my mom." "Hello Mrs. Dawson, it's such a pleasure to meet you." said Linda. "You as well dear," as she reached out to hug Linda. "Sorry baby, but we hug in this family; we give love everyday all day." "Oh yeah, I forgot to tell you, my entire family will expect hugs when they meet you," said Blake. "No problem, I wish my family did that," said Linda. "Where is dad?" asked Blake. "He's out back on the grill," said Blake's mom. As Blake and Linda made their way through the house and eventually to the back yard, every person she met gave her a big hug – just as told by Blake.

Linda was so happy for the affection she was receiving from all Blake's family. Linda came from a very dry and boring family. No one hugged and there were no kisses nor I love you from time to time. Linda was pleasantly surprised by Blake's family and this made him even more attractive to her. Linda spent most of her time in the kitchen with Blake's mom and aunts - cooking, having girl talk and plenty of laughs. The ladies in the kitchen were drinking champagne as they cooked and told stories about anything and everything. Blake spent most of his time outside with his dad and a few of his male cousins talking about women and sports. It was a typical black family cookout with plenty of great food, liquor and dancing. Blake was having such a good time with his dad and cousins he didn't even realize that Linda had disappeared for the past hour or so. He went looking for her to make sure she was okay, only to find her in the kitchen with a bunch of females getting twisted from the champagne. "Hey ladies, don't be getting my date drunk in this kitchen" Blake said laughing. "Too late, she has already had five glasses of champagne, so five more glasses won't matter," said his mom. All the women started laughing and politely told Blake goodbye.

Linda was in heaven, she had never experienced such a warm tight knitted family. Linda's personality fit right in with Blake's mom and all her sisters. She was more convinced now than ever that she had stumbled onto something special with this guy. As the event was coming to an end, Blake and Linda were two of the last guests to leave.

They stayed to help clean up and made sure everything was back in place before leaving. "Well, I think that's everything" said Blake. "Thanks for everything son." By the way, that's a real nice young lady you got there boy, don't fuck it up!" said Blake's dad. "Whatever!" said Blake. "No, seriously, you can tell she is a classy chick. You don't find girls like her everyday son, if you know what I mean" said Blake's dad. "Yes sir", said Blake. "I think you know that, that's why you brought her to the house. I know I taught you about quality - that's quality" said Blake's dad. "I hear you poppy," said Blake. "Alright, I'm done with it, if you want to be stupid, it's all up to you" said Blake's dad. "Poppy, I'm listening to you, trust me," said Blake. "Well Ms. Dawson, I think the kitchen, dining room and bathroom are all clean," said Linda. "Linda, thank you so much for coming. I've enjoyed your company so much today and I so look forward to seeing you at many more events we will have in the future" said Blake's mom. "It was my pleasure Mrs. Dawson, you have such a great family; it's hard not to have a good time. Even though I think I drank a little too much champagne today," said Linda. "Baby, what you drank today is nothing compared to what we normally drink. Trust me," said Blake's mom as she laughed and gave Linda a big hug.

Blake drove to the Burger King where Linda's car was parked. Once they arrived, Blake asked Linda if she was okay to drive but her response was so slurred that without hesitation he drove to his house. Linda never said a word, in fact; she fell asleep along the 15 minute ride to Blake's apartment. Blake realized Linda couldn't hang with his mom and aunts when it came to drinking. Upon arrival, Blake helped Linda from the car and into his apartment. Blake took Linda to his bedroom so she could rest. He knew she was twisted and would probably go straight to sleep. Linda fell asleep with all her clothes on. While she slept,

Blake took the opportunity to admire her beauty. Blake later took a shower and went to bed.

Linda woke up about 5:00 am. She started looking around the room trying to figure where she was. She saw Blake lying next to her and was extremely happy that he was such a gentleman allowing her sleep without trying anything. Linda stared at Blake for a couple minutes as he slept; the covers had slid down to his stomach so she could really see his chest and arms. Blake had a body similar to the model Tyson Beckford. Blake, being an athlete all his life stayed in great shape. Even at 32 years old, Blake still had a six pack and biceps of someone who went to the gym daily. Linda eased out the bed and went to the bathroom while Blake slept.

Linda couldn't help but noticing that Blake had a linen closet inside the bathroom, which was rare. Inside the closet he had a pack of brand new tooth brushes; so she helped herself to one. Linda took her clothes off and went to have a quick shower since she hadn't bathed since the day before. As Linda was taking her shower she heard a voice – "May I join you?" Startled by the question, Linda didn't respond because she was actually brushing her teeth when the question was posed. "May I join you?" said the voice again. "Sure, it's your house." Blake was excited about the response and did not hesitate to enter the shower with Linda. Linda was feeling rather nervous at this situation but played it cool. Linda looked at this 6'2" chocolate-toned man entering the shower with an amazingly chiseled body. Blake looking at Linda's ass as he entered the shower was thinking "Oh my goodness!" Linda had an ass like that of Serena Williams. It was a great way to start the day seeing a body like hers. Linda and Blake were both intrigued by the other's body, which made the shower experience more interesting. Blake asked Linda if he could move to the front in order for him to brush his teeth. Linda obliged, and both were totally checking out each other as they moved about in the shower. They were both pleased with the other's body that their thoughts were about to be put into action. Linda noticed that Blake's dick was getting erect when he moved to the front to brush his teeth. She didn't know if that happened because of him seeing her ass or whether, as most men they would wake up with a hard dick.

At that point, it didn't matter because Blake's dick was looking wonderful to her. After Blake brushed his teeth, he turned to Linda and leaned towards her. She was ready and waiting for it. Blake kissed Linda so passionately - the water from the shower hitting both their faces made the kissing sexier than ever. As they were kissing, Linda started stroking Blake's dick as Blake was playing with Linda's pussy with his fingers. Blake turned Linda around and put her hands on the towel rack to the back of the shower. Blake, slowly penetrated Linda from behind as the water was beating on her back. Blake stroked and caressed her 36 D breasts which felt so good in his hands. They were doing this for several minutes before he turned the shower off and stepped out to grab a towel and dried Linda. Once he finished with Linda, he dried himself then walked in the bedroom where Linda was already waiting. As Blake walked into the room, he saw Linda standing before the bed looking through the window. Linda's entire body, from the soles of her feet to the tips of her fingers to the wet hair of her pussy was wanting him so badly, and Blake knew it. Blake walked over to Linda, turned her towards him and gave her the gentlest kiss ever. The kiss was so soft and sensual it made her pussy wet and her nipples harden instantly.

Blake picked Linda up and carried her to the middle of the bed where he spread her legs as widely as they could get. It was now easy for him to begin eating her pussy and this he did like a thirsty man in a dessert. He licked her clitoris like it had never been done before. He licked it for several moments and then gently sucked on it until she exploded like a gusher of water from a boat with a massive leak.

Blake then gave Linda some serious dick for the next 20 minutes while sucking her breast in the process. Linda came twice during the encounter.

Blake and Linda were fucking so hard and both parties were enjoying it. It was a surprise the bed had not caught fire with all the heat generated by the two. They were really getting it on. When Linda came for the fourth time, Blake came with her; they both knew this was something special. Blake went and turned the shower back on and asked Linda to join him. Linda was truly feeling like, this might be my Mr. Right or Mr. Right-Now. Either way, Linda and Blake were enjoying each other to the fullest. After they got out of the shower, Blake went to the kitchen and started preparing eggs and bacon while Linda stayed in bed watching TV. Blake popped open a bottle of Moet and took Linda a glass to sip until breakfast was ready. Blake brought Linda a plate with the best looking cheese and eggs and perfectly cooked bacon with buttered toast. Linda was so impressed with Blake's cooking skills.

"Okay, who are you?" asked Linda. "What do you mean by that?" asked Blake. "You look good, you fucked me great, you're a total gentleman in and out of bed, you have an amazing family and your black ass can cook. So I say again, who the hell are you? and what have I gotten myself into?" said Linda. "I'm just a black man who is trying his best to make you smile," said Blake. "Yea right." said Linda.

Blake would see Linda from time to time over the next month. For Linda, all she could do was think about Blake, while at work Linda was thinking- I can hear the sound of his balls slapping against my pussy, I wish he was inside me right now. I wish that I was sitting on his dick, with my back to him, rocking back and forth as I sit here at my computer. A sister can get a lot of work done that way. When he fucks me, a feeling comes over me that I cannot quite express. I shiver but I feel calm at the same time. No man has ever made me feel so desired, like he is so pleased by my efforts. He always gives me a serious dick down and I do mean dick down. He ate my pussy until I detonated all over his tongue. It was such an amazing feeling. I wished that I could fuck him twenty-four seven. If I could, I would walk around with his dick in my ass; in my pussy; in my mouth. Ooh, yes, definitely in my mouth. Damn, I hope he comes over tonight so we can 'cum' together like there was no tomorrow. I pray he comes, so he can bury his dick into me balls deep and put me to sleep like a baby."

For Blake, even though he enjoyed himself, it was "just another day at the office". Blake was fortunate enough to meet some outstanding women, who most men would marry in two seconds. However, for Blake, Brandi still had his heart and no matter whom he met or fucked, that wasn't changing.

A month had gone by and Blake was pretty much over Linda. Linda would call and Blake would either not answer or text her to say he was busy, but wouldn't return the call. Linda got the hint and stopped calling. She was very disappointed that she couldn't get Blake to feel for her the way she felt for him.

CHAPTER 4

A Needed Apology

Two months later, Blake's family was having another get-together for Labor Day and Blake was on his way to the event. Blake had met a new woman right after he stopped seeing Linda and decided to take her to the event. However, when Blake pulled up to his parents' house, he recognized Linda's Honda Accord parked in the driveway. As he slowly approached, his cousin Mike came to the driver's window to greet him.

"Blake, what up dude?" "Hey Mike, who in the house?" asked Blake. At that moment, Mike gave Blake the man code look that meant "Don't take your black ass in that house with that girl in your car!!"

"Got it!" said Blake.

Blake told his date he forgot something at his house and kept going. His date didn't question the situation. Blake was totally pissed off, trying to figure why Linda would be at his parents' house. The next day, Blake called his mom to ask why Linda was at the house. "Ma, yesterday I came to the house for the function and saw Linda's car there. What was she doing at the house?" asked Blake. "What do you mean? I invited her," said his mom. "Ma, why would you invite Linda to the house without checking with me first?" said Blake. "Boy, this is my house, why do I have to check with you about who I invite to my house?" Ma, you know I'm not seeing Linda anymore and I had a date with me in the car and for that reason I couldn't come in. That would have been a very crazy scene," said Blake. "That's on you son, she and I are friends, you not dating her is your business," said his mom. "Ma, how can you in your right mind think it's okay to have women that I used to see at your house? In fact, you only saw her twice so when did she become such a good friend of yours? I only saw her for a month myself," said Blake. "Son, I'm not going to argue with you about who can come to my house, you get it?" said his mom. "Okay Ma, if that's how you feel - don't expect to see me at your house ever again, and I mean that. If you are willing to put a stranger before your son, so be it," take care and have a nice day." said Blake.

For the following two months, Blake never went to his parents' house and missed several family gatherings. Everyone kept asking his mom where he was. Whenever she explained what happened, everyone, especially Blake's dad told her how wrong she was. It didn't hit home until her closest sister Judy told her that she should have checked with him to see if he would have a problem with her being there, since they were no longer seeing each other. In fact, Judy said Linda should have called Blake herself and told him that his mom had invited her over, to see if he would have a problem with it. Judy told her sister she should not have put her son in that situation and that she owed him an apology.

Judy knew that Blake was a man of his word, and when he said something, he meant it. On top of that, everyone was mad at Blake's mom for making him feel like he couldn't come to his parents' house anymore. Blake was always the life of the party and things were so different without his presence, especially for his dad. Blake and his dad had a very close relationship, so Blake's mom knew she had to do something to fix it. After talking with Judy, Blake's mom called him and apologized and everything went back to normal.

However, Blake pledged to himself that from that day on, he would never take a girl to a family event unless she was going to be his wife. It's funny how family members (especially women) could become so attached to someone they had just met. Men are so not like that. Blake's dad would never have invited a dude to the house after his nieces had stopped dating them. Men don't encourage those thoughts or actions.

CHAPTER 5

A Private Party

Early one Saturday morning, Preach called Blake to see if he would go with him to a private party. Preach told Blake that there was a new connect he needed that would be at the party. Preach liked having Blake at his side at functions with college educated people who also dabbled in the drug world. These types of functions were all about making people comfortable with each other, so doing business would not be a problem. Blake served as the face to his uncle's supply source. Preach was not a book educated man, he was a street educated hustler, and if you didn't know him, his presence was extremely intimidating. Preach was not good on the eyes but had great gift of gab, especially with the ladies.

Even though Preach wasn't the best looking man, he got plenty of trim and women loved him, so he was doing something right. One could tell from the time they walked into the event, which was held at the Grand Hyatt in the Presidential suite, that this was the upper crust of the drug trade. They had servers who brought champagne on the arrival of patrons. The champagne of choice for this crowd was "Cristal" which cost around $250 per bottle. There was an endless supply for this group, and along with a catered buffet that consisted of fried catfish, spiced shrimp that were already peeled, sautéed spinach with creamed cheese, lobster tails, collard greens, barbecued chicken wings and T-bone steaks which had an out-of-this-world sauce; there was also a table with salad and multiple desserts to suit anyone's taste buds. The average person would have lost his mind in this setting, but Blake was cool as iced water, hence the reason Preach made sure Blake was always at his side at these affairs. Conversely, Preach was very uncomfortable at these types of affairs. He was your typical hood rat that loved being with beautiful women and making money. Preach loved boxing and gambling. He never missed a big fight in Las Vegas and loved to hit the crap tables while he was there.

When Sugar Ray fought Tommy Hearns for the title; Preach won $75K shooting dice that night in Vegas. There was one thing Blake admired about his uncle - even though he was not good on the eyes, before the night was over, Preach would always get the best looking girl. Blake built his confidence from these situations, just watching his uncle at work. He knew from watching Preach, that any man could get any woman once he knew what to say. As the party got into full gear, Preach told Blake that he desperately needed to meet a gentleman named "Ricco". Preach told Blake that Ricco could change the game for him because of his product and price; as, currently, Preach was getting his product from someone who was getting it from Ricco and Preach wanted to cut the middle man out and get his supplies directly from the source. In doing so, he could increase his revenues by 50%.

Blake could tell that Ricco was a force in the room by the way everyone was catering to him and kissing his ass for no apparent reason. Blake told his uncle Preach there was something about that Ricco he didn't like. Preach told Blake to keep his personal feelings in check, this was business and it was always advisable never allow personal feelings to interfere with business.

Preach finally made his way over to Ricco and introduced himself and his nephew Blake. "Hello sir, I'm Preach and this is my nephew Blake." "You're Preach? Ronny has mentioned your name to me from time to time. Is Ronny treating you okay, any problems?" "Everything is okay, but it could be a whole lot better," said Preach. "What do you mean?"

asked Ricco. "Ronny is not always responsive to my needs and waiting costs me money. However, if I was dealing directly with you, I believe I could put more money in my pockets as well as yours" replied Preach. "Does this waiting happen often?" asked Ricco. "Too often for me, I have too many people waiting on product and to be out of stock for three maybe five days is torture" said Preach. "Ronny told me you were the best person in his crew," said Ricco. "Maybe that's the problem," said Blake. That statement sent shock waves through Ricco and Preach.

"My uncle doesn't need a middle man to hinder his business, just think how much you would hate that situation," said Blake. Preach had a very nervous look on his face while Blake was talking. Preach felt that Blake was speaking to Ricco with a little disrespect for someone he was just meeting. However, to Preach's surprise, Ricco actually respected what Blake was saying and agreed to deal with Preach directly. "Preach, here is my cell number, whenever you need product, text me with '99' and I will have someone get to you within the hour. Never call my cell number, once I see '99' someone will text you an address to meet them by the next hour. Does this work for you?" asked Ricco. "Hell yea," said Preach. What do you normally spend on a kilo with Ronny?" asked Ricco. "$30K." said Preach. "Your new price is

$25K, thank your nephew for that gift," said Ricco as he walked away.

Blake was now sensing very bad vibes both from and towards Ricco. He didn't know why - normally, Blake would not have cared about whom Preach was doing business with. However, for some reason, this situation was different, Blake just didn't know why. When Preach and Blake left the party, Preach grabbed Blake and gave him a big hug. "You did it young fella, you did it!! Wow, you were losing me when you first started talking to Ricco; you were talking like you hated the man. I've never seen you that way with these dudes. Anyway, you made my situation much better, no more waiting for product and much more profit. I owe you big time for this one young fella!! If everything goes well, I will be rich and ready for retirement within 5 years, trust me." said Preach.

On the ride home, Blake asked Preach a lot of questions about Ricco. Preach could only tell him what he had heard because that was his first time meeting him. Preach told Blake that he heard he drove a silver Bentley; was a dentist and had a young wife who was a computer whiz. He heard they lived in Potomac, Maryland in a gated community with the filthy rich people.

Preach went on to talk about the un-assuming persons who were now involved in the drug game – people who were least expected. On the ride home,

PREACH

Ronny called Preach and told him he heard that he was no longer on his team. Ronny was very mad at Preach for approaching Ricco and jumping ship. Ronny told Preach "payback is a bitch!" Preach knew that meant he should watch his back. Preach knew that Ronny was mad because he is now missing out on the $5K extra per kilo he was charging Preach. Ronny also knew with the new connection Preach now has, he would become very large in the game. Ronny was keeping Preach on a leash by allowing him to only make a certain amount of money. Ronny could have supplied Preach more product but he was afraid Preach would get too large and move past him in the food chain.

Preach was buying 4 kilo a month from Ronny for $120K, now he was able to get 5 kilos for almost the same price and make an extra $75K a month. Not bad for a small time hood rat from Barry Farms.

It was now apparent to Blake, the reason for the invited guests to be sucking up to Ricco at the party. The new connect that was made between Preach and Ricco, had Preach, Gary and some of Blake's other cousins making more money than ever. Preach and his nephews went from 5 kilos a month to 10 kilos a month.

Everyone was raising their game and doing big things now that they had more income. Gary was Blake's closest cousin who had recently moved into a penthouse suite in a fancy building in Southwest, near the waterfront. Gary was a carbon copy of Blake without the education. Gary was a smooth brother with the ladies but knew how to handle himself on the streets. He was like Dr. Jekyll and Mr. Hide. On one hand Gary was one of the most generous dudes one would ever meet, then on the other hand, if you crossed him in any way, he could easily put a bullet to your brain and go home to sleep like a baby. You may want to always be on Gary's good side or it could mean lights out for you.

Gary had murdered a few people during rough times, however, he was very calculating with everything he did, meaning, if Gary decided to kill anyone, they would never see it coming and no one would ever find out about it. The person would just disappear from the neighborhood, without a trace. Once, Gary was at the movies with one of many female friends and this dude kept talking during the movie and Gary's friend was getting fed up with the guy and asked him kindly to lower his voice. The dude's response was "Fuck you bitch!" Needless to say, he had no idea who he was dealing with. Gary didn't say a word and this surprised his date. Two minutes later, the dude got up and headed for the men's room. Gary told his date he would be right back, ten minutes later, Gary came back and sat down and finished watching the movie. Gary's date was so relieved that the dude never came back inside the theatre and they were able to watch the movie in peace.

The next day on the news, there was a reported homicide that occurred at the same theatre Gary and his date were. Gary's date saw the news and told Gary about it. She told him the description of the person fit the guy who called her bitch. She said that they found the dude in one of the theatres that wasn't being used the night they went to the movies. The cause of death was still unknown at the time of broadcast. This definitely made Gary's date wonder if he had something to do with what happened when he was gone for ten minutes, but she let it go and never mentioned it again.

As I said before, with Gary, everything was calculated. Risk vs. Reward. Gary and Blake would hang out often at Gary's new place. Gary had one of his "dimes" decorate the place and it was furnished as a typical basketball player's pad. Gary even had a pool table in the unit, which was the way he and Blake spent most of their time. They played pool for money every time Blake passed through. Blake was a better pool player than Gary, but from time to time, Gary would come out on top. When Gary knew Blake would be stopping by, he made sure he had a couple dimes there for them to enjoy. Gary and Blake had the same taste in women so Blake was always pleased with the girls that would be at Gary's crib.

CHAPTER 6

The New found Love

There was this girl named Tiffany who Blake was very fond of. He had met her at Gary's crib. Tiffany was the sister of one of Gary's many females. Gary had met them at the car wash on Branch Avenue one day and invited them both over for dinner. Gary was not a good cook but he could order out with the best of them. Whenever Gary wanted to impress a female, he would drive to three different restaurants and ordered the best entrée on the menu, go home and used the cooking pans as if he cooked it. He would at times, hire a chef to prepare the meal for the evening. This heavily depended on how special the female was or how special he wanted her to feel. Gary was a true player but always a gentleman with the ladies. This is why Gary and Blake were so close; they were alike in so many ways. When they were growing up, everything between the two was always a competition, from who could get the 'baddest' girl, or who could play sports better, to who would do better in school.

The competitive nature pushed both to do better in life. Gary was a very good student and an ideal candidate for college. Unfortunately for Gary, he got caught up into the drug world as a result of his dad and brothers; whereas Blake had a different example in his house. Blake's parents both worked for Metro and instilled a great work ethic in him.

Truth be told, Gary was much smarter than Blake in school and Blake knew it. Blake just caught the breaks in life and Gary didn't. Gary's life was predicated on the circumstances around him. His mom was a single parent with six kids, and even though his dad sold drugs, the fruits of that labor didn't always make it in Gary's household. As a result, Gary and his brothers did what they had to do to ensure they had food, shelter and some of the good things in life. Gary and his brothers have been caught selling drugs on several occasions by the police; however, no one ever served more than a year in jail. Gary's longest stint in jail was five months, and for this reason, he never made it to college.

Gary wanted to go to college so badly because Blake had gotten a full scholarship to the University of Florida and he knew that Blake was winning in the competitive nature of their relationship. To Gary's mind, he felt like he was finally on Blake's level in life. It is funny how money has a way of giving people a false sense of reality and accomplishments. Blake had a respectable job, a college degree and great foundation to achieve the American dream. However, regardless of those achievements, Gary felt since he now had more money than Blake, a much better house and car, he was now winning the game between the two. These were thoughts that went on in Gary's mind; Blake let those thoughts go when he went to college. In Blake's mind, Gary was his favorite cousin and he wanted to see him do well in life. Blake knew what Gary had been through to get to where he was; so Blake always had his back, no matter what.

Most of the girls that Blake met at Gary's place were just something to do for the moment; hit it a few times and let it go. However, when Blake met Tiffany, she didn't fit into the typical box of women for Blake. There was something special about this young lady. She was well educated, very attractive and worked in the finance world just like Blake. The icing on the cake was that Tiffany was a sports fanatic. When they met during dinner at Gary's place, Tiffany asked if they could eat in the living room because the game was on. That blew Blake's mind because he was mad he was missing the game trying to be nice. So when Tiffany made the statement, Blake's attraction to her went up 1000%. Blake thought to himself, "Wow, beautiful, sexy, smart and loves sports, it doesn't get better than this for me." Blake was now in heaven for the rest of the evening with his new found friend. Gary had three bedrooms in his penthouse and by the end of the evening, Blake would normally be in one smashing whoever was there at the time, but with Tiffany, Blake was totally content just talking with her. Tiffany and Blake talked until 5:00 am before they both fell asleep on the floor before the TV. Gary woke up around 5:15am to get some water from the kitchen and found Blake and Tiffany sleeping on the floor. Gary was in total shock; Blake had never done something like this with a female he met at Gary's place. Gary thought to himself "Oh shit, Blake has caught the bug." Gary was right, for the first time in his life; he had never seen Blake act like this towards a young lady. Let's not get it twisted, Blake had met many smoking hot chicks at Gary's place; most of them had the same attributes as Tiffany except the sports aspect. Gary knew Blake felt something special for Tiffany. Tiffany pushed all the right buttons with Blake. After that night, Blake and Tiffany were inseparable. Every time Blake came to Gary's house, Tiffany was on his arm. Blake even called Gary to thank him for the introduction and to ask him not to invite him over to the 'crib' when other girls were there. Blake told Gary that Tiffany was the one for him and that he was totally content with seeing where their relationship would go.

During their courtship, Blake wined and dined Tiffany like she was his new bride. He cooked dinner for her, took her shopping and his favorite thing with her was going to the Lincoln Memorial and sitting on the steps with a bottle of Moet and two cheeseburgers. Tiffany also enjoyed that very much.

Tiffany had never met a man like Blake; she thought Blake was the ultimate gentleman. The main thing about Blake that blew her mind was that Blake never tried to have sex with her. At the end of the evening, Blake would drive her home, walk her to the door, kiss her on the lips very gently and say goodnight. This went on for several months and it drove Tiffany crazy. She started thinking Blake wasn't sexually attracted to her. All types of crazy things started going through Tiffany's mind after the second month with no attempts to have sex with her. However, Tiffany knew what she was bringing to the table; she had a body like Lisa Raye and a face like Halle Berry. Tiffany had never dated a man or even went out with a brother who didn't try to get the cookie within two days. Now, here she possibly had the man of her dreams not trying to get the "cookie". Tiffany was totally confused by Blake's actions or non-actions, some would say. A part of Tiffany was happy that he was taking his time with her but then the other part of her wanted so badly to fuck him, it was driving her crazy. Blake on the other hand felt like Tiffany was special, so he wanted to treat her like she was special and not rush into anything. Blake knew Tiffany didn't know his track record with women, but, he wanted to prove to himself that he could take his time and get to know this woman before sex came into the picture.

Blake knew based on his past experiences, if he had sex with Tiffany too soon, he wouldn't value her and would probably put her in the same category as the other bombshells he had been with. Blake knew he was taking a risk by holding back sex from the gorgeous black female.

However, risk vs reward made him see the big picture and Blake had decided that Tiffany was a part of his big picture. After dating for four months, with Tiffany ready to slit her wrist over Blake not touching her like she wanted to be touched; Tiffany decided to take matters into her own hands. Tiffany called Blake at work to see if he was free for the weekend. After getting the green light from Blake, Tiffany planned the most romantic weekend at the Marriott, in downtown DC. Tiffany asked Blake if she could pick him up from his apartment because she had a surprise for him. Blake knew she was up to something, he just didn't know what it was. Tiffany went to the mall on her lunch break to get her ammunition for the weekend. She had made the hotel reservation that morning after thinking about how she so badly wanted Blake to caress her entire body for a couple days. Tiffany was a good girl and hadn't had sex for almost a year. After all the wining and dining Blake was doing with her, her hormonal juices were flowing and really wanted Blake to have her in every way possible. Tiffany picked Blake up from his apartment at 6pm sharp, when he got in the car; Blake asked, "What are you up to?" "I just want to do something special for you this weekend, since you're always spoiling me, it's your turn," said Tiffany. "You said weekend, does this mean I'm not going back home tonight?" asked Blake. "That would be correct sir," said Tiffany. "What about clothes and a toothbrush?" asked Blake. "I got you covered, trust me," said Tiffany with a devilish grin on her face. "Oh, by the way, you have 15 minutes to use your phone for the rest of the weekend," said Tiffany. "What?" asked Blake. "You heard me, in 15 minutes we will be at our destination and both you and I will turn off our phones and leave them in the car. Can you handle that?" said Tiffany. "Sounds like I don't have a choice." said Blake. "That would be correct sir," said Tiffany. "Have you ever not used a cell phone for two days?" asked Tiffany. "When I got sick some time ago said Blake. "Well, this time it's going to be a choice that we both make," said Tiffany. Blake was now very curious to see what Tiffany had up her sleeve.

As Tiffany was driving, Blake kept trying to figure out where she was taking him, but with every turn she made, Blake didn't have a clue, until she made a right turn into the entrance of the Marriott Hotel. Now Blake was wondering what was going on. He hadn't heard about any event they were having, so his mind kept racing with different thoughts. As they pulled up in front of the hotel, Tiffany popped the trunk of her car so the valet could get her luggage. "Why do you have luggage and I have nothing?" asked Blake. "Trust me Blake, I got you," said Tiffany.

Tiffany led Blake through the lobby to room 777, which was a junior executive suite that was set up like a duplex (meaning, it had an upstairs apartment). Blake and Tiffany walked in the suite. Upon entering, the suite had a long L- shaped leather couch with a dining room table that seated eight people. There was a beautifully decorated bathroom to the left of the dining room and a balcony that overlooked the entire Washington Monument and to the right of that was a spectacular view of the Lincoln Memorial. As Blake stepped to the balcony, he remarked "Wow, this view is breath-taking." "Yes it is." said Tiffany. "Are you ready to go?" asked Tiffany. "Go where?" asked Blake. "You will see," said Tiffany. Blake and Tiffany headed back downstairs to the lobby and got in a waiting cab in front of the hotel. "701 Pennsylvania Ave, please," said Tiffany to the cab driver. Within 4 minutes, they were at the location.

Tiffany walked Blake who was now puzzled as hell to the exclusive "701" restaurant. Blake had heard about that restaurant for years, but never had the opportunity to go there. Tiffany and Blake walked in and the hostess approached them "names please?" "Mr. Dawson," answered Tiffany. "Right this way please," said the hostess. Blake was impressed that Tiffany had gone out of her way to create a special weekend for the two. Normally, Blake would be the one initiating romantic events. Now, for once, it was his turn to lay back and let whatever happens, happen. After being seated, the waiter immediately brought a bottle of Moet to the table and an order of caviar. This blew Blake's mind, these were two of his favorite things in the world. "Wow! You either really know me well or you have seriously done your research," said Blake. "I would say a little of both," said Tiffany. Tiffany had preordered the entire meal and everything that came was Blake's favorite. The entrée consisted of stuffed flounder with crabmeat, shrimp and scallops, sautéed cream spinach and Jasmine rice with sprinkles of bacons. The meal blew Blake's mind. "I'm trying to figure out how you knew exactly what to order for me. Everything was perfect!" said Blake. "A girl can get lucky from time to time," said Tiffany with a devilish grin on her face. After talking for another 20 minutes, Tiffany asked Blake if he was ready to go, Blake looked a little puzzled because no one had brought the check to the table. "We have to pay dinner, right?" asked Blake. "I've already taken care of that," said Tiffany with a big smile on her face. "You are enjoying this, aren't you," asked Blake. "Yes I am, surprisingly, I never knew you could be so enjoyable. Let's go." said Tiffany. This time, instead of catching a cab back to the hotel, Blake and Tiffany walked back, talking and laughing about anything and everything. Tiffany had definitely created a very romantic evening so far, and Blake was in heaven with her efforts. The walk was good for them, because it presented a chance to walk that dinner off their bodies and not feel so bloated. In recent times walking and talking had become Tiffany and Blake's favorite past time. When they got back to the suite, Tiffany asked Blake to go upstairs and take a shower; Blake obliged, but while he was in the shower, Tiffany got in with him which he found very surprising. "OMG, is today my birthday and I forgot?" Blake asked jokingly. "For me, every day is your birthday, so enjoy everything that's happening and ask no question," said Tiffany. Both Blake and Tiffany were admiring each other's body in the shower, they both knew they would be happy when this moment came and they both were correct.

Tiffany grabbed the wash cloth from Blake and began washing his entire body. Blake loved every minute of it. He felt convicted to return the favor. They were totally aroused in the shower and wanted so badly to make love to each other.

As Blake was about to make his move, Tiffany said "I need you downstairs now." "Are you serious?" asked Blake. At this moment, all Blake could think about was finally making love to Tiffany. His dick was so hard it began hurting. Out of curiosity, Blake went along with the program and grabbed one of two robes on the back of the door and headed downstairs. To his surprise, there were two massage tables set up in the living room area with a masseuse standing in front of each awaiting their arrival. They had turned the lights out and lit candles to set the right mood. There was soft ocean music being played but Blake couldn't tell where the music was coming from.

Tiffany came down stairs right after Blake; she wanted Blake to get the surprise before she came down. There, sitting on the dining table, was a bottle of Moet chilling on ice with two champagne glasses. Blake and Tiffany got on their individual massage table and began to get their massages. Blake's mind was now on fire, Tiffany's stock just went through the roof.

No woman had ever treated Blake this good. This was the first time that a woman had ever spent money on Blake. Tiffany and Blake thoroughly enjoyed their side by side massages. Once the two masseuses had left the suite, Tiffany poured two glasses of champagne and grabbed some chocolate covered strawberries she had in the refrigerator. She brought them to Blake who was lying on the couch and then she headed upstairs. Blake grabbed the remote control and turned on a NBA game. After a few minutes, Tiffany joined Blake downstairs – She was wearing a shear white teddy from Victoria Secret. Blake immediately sat up on the couch. Tiffany walked over and stood in front of him allowing him to take it all in. Without hesitation, Blake stood and put his arms around her. He stared into her eyes for what seemed like forever – he allowed his eyes to do all the talking. After that powerful gaze, Blake gave Tiffany the most passionate kiss she ever had; he moved his tongue in her mouth ever so gently that the kiss had Tiffany on the verge of climaxing. Blake then picked Tiffany up and carried her to the dining room table. He sat her on the table and directed her back to lean against the wall. Blake began kissing Tiffany's inner thighs and went down to her knees and began sucking her toes. Blake sucked one toe at a time as if they were not related. He then made his way to her thighs again. Blake discovered that Tiffany's inner thighs were one of her sensitive spots. He spent more time with the inner thighs because of the reactions he was receiving.

He eventually moved towards her pussy area where things became even more interesting. Blake moved Tiffany's crotch area of her teddy to the side so he could lick her pussy. With the first lick, Tiffany was "cummin", her body was so worked up from Blake licking her inner thighs and him licking her pussy that it made her explode. "God damn, damn, damn, damn, damn," Tiffany kept saying as she was "cummin". Blake was smiling with happiness as Tiffany was "cummin". As Tiffany lay on the table, Blake took a dining room chair to the balcony and came back for Tiffany. Blake stripped Tiffany of her shear teddy and headed to the balcony to continue. Blake sat in the chair and Tiffany straddled him so they were facing each other. Tiffany sat on Blake's dick and when she did, you could see a sense of relief over her face. It was if her face said, "Finally, thank you Jesus!" Blake felt the same way, Tiffany's pussy was warm and juicy and fit Blake's dick like a glove. Their love making was as if it was written and directed for a movie scene – It was epic, passionate, and explosive all at the same time. Other than Brandi, Blake finally let go and allowed his heart to feel for someone else. Tiffany on the other hand was being very cautious with Blake, she felt either Blake was too good to be true or she was having a wonderful dream that would end when she woke up. Either way, from that moment, everything would change. Blake was falling hard and for the second time in his life, he couldn't control it. Tiffany had put the "mojo" on this black man and he embraced it. Every day after their encounter, Blake woke up thinking about Tiffany and throughout the day he thought about her.

After their weekend, Tiffany called her sister and expressed her feelings. She told her sister that Blake possessed all the qualities she was looking for in a man and confessed that there were things about Blake that had her puzzled.

Tiffany realized that everything Blake was doing for her and the way he lived was above his income level, so she figured something was going on but she just didn't know how to put her fingers on it. She explained to her sister about the lavish gifts he would give her, and the expensive getaway weekend trips they had taken over the past six months, not to mention his daily lifestyle. Tiffany was a very sharp young lady who like Blake possessed a financial background, so she could easily discern when someone was living above their means, and Blake clearly lived like someone who made much more than his legal income represented. Even though Tiffany was on full alert with Blake's lifestyle, she was totally committed to the way he treated her and the way he carried himself in and out of the bedroom. Tiffany wanted so badly to ask Blake about the extra income that he possessed, but didn't want to offend him in any way. She knew that for her peace of mind, she had to know.

One evening Blake was chilling at Tiffany's crib and he started talking to her about his plan of taking her to Aruba for her birthday. Tiffany decided this would be the perfect opportunity to bring up the lavish lifestyle Blake was living without the visible mean to do so. "Blake, can I ask you a question without you getting upset?" asked Tiffany. "Sure, what is it?" said Blake. "Where are you getting all this money to live the way you do?" asked Tiffany. "All what money?" asked Blake. "Let's see, during my third month of knowing you, you took me to the Bahamas and Las Vegas. While in Las Vegas, you brought me this beautiful tennis bracelet that's on my wrist right now, and I know jewelry- this is not cheap. I know we went to dinner at least ten times during that month, with each dinner costing over $100 a pop. Last month, you took me shopping in Miami and Atlanta. I know you spent at least $10k in Miami, because you spent $6K on clothes and spa treatments just for me. Don't get me wrong, I absolutely love being treated this way, no man has ever done the things you do with me. I'm just concerned about your source of funds - where is the money coming from to do all this? I also know your America Express bill is at least $10 to $15K every month; because I very rarely see you using cash. Everything you do is with your

American Express card. So be real with me and tell me what's up," said Tiffany. "Wow, you are good, your calculation of what I've been spending is on point. I forgot you are a financial wizard like me," Blake said while laughing. "Stop stalling and tell me what's going on, please." said Tiffany.

"I have an uncle and some cousins who dabble in the drug business. They make a ton of money and come to me for advice on investment options and for my services I charge them a fee." said Blake. "They must make a lot of money," said Tiffany. "They do" said Blake. "So to be crystal clear Mr. Dawson, are you implying that you do not sell drugs with your uncle and cousins?" asked Tiffany. "I swear to you Tiffany, I do not sell drugs," said Blake with much conviction. At that moment, Tiffany hugged Blake and said "Thank you for being honest with me." Blake thought to himself that only 80% of what he said was actually true.

Tiffany and Blake continued their enjoyable evening and the conversation was never mentioned again. However, that conversation had Blake thinking a lot about Tiffany and his feelings for her, so the next day, Blake took the day off and went uptown and purchased a beautiful 2 carat engagement ring for her. He wasn't quite sure when he would give it to her, but he knew she was the woman for him and at some point in the near future, he would propose to her. He just needed a little more time to make sure he was making the right move.

After purchasing the ring, Blake called his uncle Preach for a meeting at his parents' house. Blake pulled up to his parents' house and two minutes later Preach pulled up. They both went in and surprised his parents with the unexpected visit. "Hey Ma, what's happening dad?" said Blake. "Hey family!" said Preach. "What are you two doing here?" asked Blake's mom. "We came to talk with Pops about something," said Blake. "Does that mean I need to leave the room?" asked Blake's mom. "If you don't mind, we won't be long" said Blake. "It must be something serious for you not to be at work," said Blake's mom.

The three men then went to the kitchen table to talk. For some strange reason most important conversations in the black community took place in the kitchen. Blake's dad and Preach were both looking at Blake trying to figure out what was so important. Blake was a little hesitant at first but came out with it. He reached into his pocket and sat the ring box on the table. "WTF, are you asking one of us to marry your dumb ass?" asked Preach rhetorically. "Whatever dude. I've been seeing this girl named Tiffany for the past six months and I do believe she is the one. That's why in recent times, I haven't been hanging out with the family much" said Blake. "Wow, my nephew is caught up in love again" said Preach. "Again, hell, when was the first time?" asked Blake's dad. "There was a cutie in college that had your son's nose wide opened", said Preach. "What happened to her?" asked his dad. "She was off limits for Blake back then" said Preach. "Can you stick to what's happening right now fellas; I wanted to run this by you two first, since you are the two that's been giving me advice since I could talk." said Blake. "Is she pretty, does she have a job, is she smart and does she have kids?" asked his dad. "She is very pretty, she has a great job, very smart and she has no kids." said Blake. "Is the pussy great and does she allow you to be the man in the house?" asked Preach, "Yes and yes" said Blake. "Sounds like a great catch. Why haven't you brought her by the house so everyone could meet her?" asked his dad. "After the last fiasco, I told you that I would never bring another female here unless she was the one, and she is the one," said Blake. "Dad, please don't tell mom until I make it official. I'm just not sure when that will be yet" said Blake.

"Mother Fucker, you buy a damn ring and you don't know when you want to give it to the chick, what's wrong with you?" asked Preach. "I have to do it when I feel the time is right," said Blake. "So, was the time right to purchase the ring?" asked his dad. Both Preach and Blake's dad started laughing at what Blake was saying, but deep down they understood. It's always a difficult decision for a man to take that step of giving a woman the ring. Sometimes, everything that is good becomes horrible after some women get the ring on their finger. Blake just wanted to be sure, but the truth is, one is never sure. Sometimes one only needs to jump from the ledge and pray to land softly - Risk vs. Reward. "This calls for a toast - where is the champagne baby boy?" asked his dad. "I have a bottle in the car, I'll get it." said Blake. The bottle of Moet was popped open and Blake's mom who heard the champagne popped open came from the back room to join the celebration. "What are we celebrating?" asked his mom. The three men looked at each other and no one said a word. "Keep your little secrets you bastards!" said his mom jokingly. Everyone laugh and continued drinking.

Blake had set up a meeting with a realtor to look at some houses in the Fort Washington area that afternoon. Blake left his parent's house and met the realtor at a house only five minutes from his parents'. It was a colonial style home with 3 bedrooms, large basement, two-car garage, swimming pool and a spacious backyard. Blake was very impressed with the house, he told the realtor he wanted to put a contract on it immediately. The realtor told Blake that the house was on the market for $350K, however, the fact that it had been on the market for months meant that the owner could consider lowering the price. The realtor said she would have a discussion with the owner on the matter. Blake and the realtor agreed to offer $275K with a passable inspection. After a week, Blake received a call from his realtor that his offer was accepted. However, during the inspection, it was discovered that the house needed a new roof, major plumbing repairs and upgraded electrical. Blake informed the realtor that he would get an estimate on the work needed and get back to her as soon as possible. Blake had many friends at his job in Georgetown who were more than capable of executing the work needed for the new home. He contacted the top electrician and plumber and took them to the residence for an estimate for the repairs. He also, contacted Virginia Roofing Company for an estimate on a new roof. To bring everything up to code would cost $25K.

Blake's realtor went back to the seller to renegotiate the selling price due to the necessary repairs needed for the bank to approve the loan. The seller agreed to lower the price to $250K and the loan was approved by the bank. Blake decided not to tell his parents nor the family about his new home until everything was completed and his house was totally set-up and ready for guests. For the next several weeks, Blake and the realtor organized the contractors needed to complete the work. Within three weeks, all the needed repairs were completed. After the final inspection, Blake went to closing on the house and everything was done, Blake was now a home owner.

After the closing, Blake called Tiffany and asked if she was available for dinner at 7:00 pm that evening. Tiffany had called Blake several times that day but Blake didn't answer because he was caught up with the closing on his house and didn't want anyone to know what he was doing. Tiffany agreed to have dinner with Blake. Blake told her that he would pick her up from her place and take her to a new restaurant that he read great reviews about. He also told her that she had to be dressed to impress for this new place. Dressing to impress was right up her alley, Tiffany loved dressing up and going out to new places; she was very excited and curious about where Blake was taking her. Blake was on time for Tiffany; the moment she entered the car Tiffany asked Blake where he was taking her. Blake never answered; instead he complimented Tiffany on the sexy blue dress she was wearing. Tiffany was confused when Blake did not make the turn to go downtown, which is where he would always take her for dinner. As hard as it was for her, Tiffany just sat there and stayed quiet while Blake drove to an unknown location. Blake drove up to this house and Tiffany was wondering who lived there. After pulling up in the drive way, Blake got out of the car and ran around to open Tiffany's door. He extended his hand to help her from the car. "Who lives here?" asked Tiffany. "A very good friend of yours" responded Blake. "A good friend of mine?" asked Tiffany. "Yes, trust me okay," said Blake. Tiffany became very suspicious now.

As Tiffany and Blake entered the premises, Tiffany was more puzzled because the house appeared completely empty. They got to the door and Blake rang the doorbell - a young black female in a waiter's outfit greeted the couple. "Welcome, Mr. Dawson and guest." Tiffany, still bewildered, greeted the young lady. She could hear nice slow music coming from another room of the house. The waitress asked the couple to follow her. She led them to the dining room where a candlelit table for two was set up as it would be in a very upscale restaurant. There was fine china with gold trim on the plates, and the silverware was all gold.

There were two exquisite champagne glasses and a bottle of Cristal chilling in a sterling silver bucket with a gold handle. The waitress seated the couple at the table and Tiffany could really hear the slow sensual music once she sat down; she looked all around the room but couldn't figure where the music was coming from and it didn't matter because many of the songs that were being played were some of her favorites. Tiffany asked Blake, "What's going on here and whose house is this?" "Just sit back, relax and let me make you smile," said Blake. "I can do that," said

Tiffany. Just as Tiffany finished that statement, the waitress brought out a tray of 2 grilled lobster tails and another tray of steamed broccoli with parmesan cheese; she told the couple this was just an appetizer. She also brought them two glasses of the best lemonade Tiffany had ever tasted in her life. The couple blessed the food and began to eat. "This food is so good," said Tiffany. Blake just sat there enjoying his food, but had a nice content smile on his face the entire time they were eating dinner. Tiffany had so many thoughts going through her head about what was happening and she really wanted to ask Blake so many questions, but didn't want to spoil whatever he had planned.

Once they were finished with the appetizer, the waitress brought out the main dish, which consisted of a mini cheese burger with mushrooms and a side order of collard greens. Tiffany was totally blown away by the choice of food that was brought to the couple. "Don't knock it until you've tried it," said Blake. Tiffany took a bite of the burger and followed it with the collard greens and was amazed by how good that combination was together. "OMG, this is surprisingly wonderful, so simple but yet so good. Who came up with this idea?" asked Tiffany. "Think about it, who doesn't love a great tasting cheeseburger?" asked Blake "Unless you don't eat meat everyone loves a great tasting burger," said

Tiffany. "Who doesn't love great collard greens that someone put their foot into?" laughed Blake. "You're absolutely right, but how did you know to put this combination together, separately they are great, I never would have thought to put them together," said Tiffany. "Do you love it?" asked Blake. "Yes…yes…yes!! I do I really do. You have totally blown me away for the past hour. This music playing is unbelievable, almost every song is my favorite and it seems like it won't stop," said Tiffany. "I'm glad you are enjoying the moment. I really put some serious thought into this date as you can see," said Blake. A particular song started playing "This is my promise, by the Temptations" and Blake asked Tiffany for a dance. "Can you bop?" asked Blake. "Of course, I'm from DC," said Tiffany. Blake and Tiffany began to dance; they were so smooth together that someone watching would have thought they had been dancing together for years. As they were dancing, Blake told Tiffany to pay attention to the words of the song. After the song, Blake took Tiffany by the hand and walked her upstairs. At this point, Tiffany was on fire, her pussy was so wet from all the romantic things Blake was doing; so in her mind, Blake was taking her somewhere in this house to give her some good loving. Blake walked Tiffany through the entire house to get her opinion about the house. While taking the tour, Tiffany was very puzzled about what was going on. After they ended up back in the dining room, Tiffany said "Please tell me what's going on Blake." "I purchased this house and I wanted you to be the first person to see it," said Blake. "Really, Wow! It's a very nice house," said Tiffany. "Thanks" said Blake. When Tiffany and Blake returned to the dining room, the bottle of Cristal was opened and two glasses were filled. Blake grabbed the two glasses and gave one to Tiffany. "To us" said Blake "To us" replied Tiffany. As she began to drink her champagne, she noticed a ring in her glass. "What is this in my glass? OMG, what is this Blake?" "It's what I hope you think it is," said Blake. Tiffany drank the entire glass just to get the ring out. "It's beautiful," said Tiffany. "Yes you are," said Blake. Blake took the ring from Tiffany's hand and got on one knee, tears started flowing immediately from Tiffany's face. "Will you do me the honor of being my wife?" asked Blake.

As Blake waited for Tiffany to answer, he noticed her hand shaking as she began to cry. Blake started getting a little concerned because Tiffany did not answer; she kept crying and staring at Blake. "Are you going to give me an answer?" asked Blake. "Yes, yes! I will marry you. I love you so much," said Tiffany. "I love you too, said Blake. This was the first time Blake has ever said those words to a female. "Do you know that's the first time you have said that to me?" asked Tiffany. "I know - falling in love doesn't come easy for me." said Blake. "By the way, this champagne is really good. What is it?" "It's Cristal. I had to make this a very special date, so I broke the piggy bank to afford this evening," said Blake in laughter. "Mrs. Future Dawson, will you decorate the house?" asked Blake. "I would love to decorate your, I mean our new house" said Tiffany with laughter. "I do have a question for you though, if you were going to ask me to marry you, why would you buy a house by yourself and not buy it with me?" asked Tiffany. "Can I be totally honest? I wasn't quite sure when I was going to ask you to marry me. I bought the ring but didn't have a set date for when I would pop the question. I've had one woman in my lifetime that captured my heart until I met you. You have made that memory disappear and for that I will forever be yours. Are you ready to go? I have something else I want you to see," said Blake. Blake and Tiffany left the house and drove downtown to the Department of Labor. It was a beautiful warm summer night and this was one of Blake's favorite places in the city to sit and talk and observe the scenery.

When they arrived, Blake went to his trunk and pulled out a big wine glass, a bottle of Cristal and a blanket. He took Tiffany by the hand and walked her up the stairs to the top step and they took a seat. "I wanted you to see one of the best views in the city. This is where I come when I need to think, have problems or want to celebrate something alone. I just want you to know this is the first time I've ever brought someone here. This has always been my place of peace, just for me. Now, I'm sharing it with you to let you know how much you mean to me", said Blake. Tiffany was very moved by the emotions that were coming from Blake; she had never seen that side of him. Tiffany always felt like there was a wall that Blake had with women. She thought there may have been someone in his past that he never got over, but, he never told her about someone special from his past and Tiffany never asked, even though she could feel it. Tiffany knew something was holding Blake back from truly giving all his love to her, but she couldn't figure out what it was. Blake and Tiffany sat on the steps and talked all night. They discussed their future together. Blake asked Tiffany not to say anything about the house until they were ready to have the family over for a family gathering of some sort. Tiffany told Blake that she would not move into the house until they were married, which Blake totally understood. Tiffany went on to explain that she has to figure out what to do with her house once they are married. Blake told her that one of the best things about them being together is that they both have financial minds that think a like when it comes to money matters. "When the time comes, we will figure it out," said Blake. As the sun came up Tiffany told

Blake that she needed to get home and get some sleep, Blake agreed. "I just want to say that yesterday was such a wonderful day and I thank you for making me smile and making my heart happy", said Tiffany. "Same here", said Blake. Blake took Tiffany home and headed to his parent's house to tell them the news. When he arrived, his mom was not there, she had an early doctor's appointment, so Blake shared the news with his dad. "Well pop, I did it" said Blake. "Did what?" asked his dad. "I proposed to Tiffany last night and she said yes," said Blake. "Wow - that was quick! You just told me and Preach that you didn't know when you were going to give her the ring. She must have really put that thing on you over these few days," said his dad. "True, true, but the moment was perfect last night, so I did it", said Blake. "I would like to invite you, ma and Preach out to dinner so you all can meet and get to know Tiffany," said Blake. "What day were you thinking about?" said his dad. "I was hoping tomorrow would work for all. I will contact Preach and find out if he will be able to make it" said Blake.

Blake contacted Preach and everything was set for dinner the next day. It was a special occasion, so Blake decided to take them to Dominique's restaurant, which happened to be Blake and Tiffany's favorite spot to dine. Dominique's was a very upscale restaurant in the city. On many occasions, celebrities and sports figures dined there because of the atmosphere and the quality of food.

Blake and Tiffany met his parents and Preach at the restaurant. Blake had called ahead and told them about the special night and requested the best table in the house. They were all seated in the main section of the restaurant in an elaborate booth where one could see everything and everyone in the restaurant. There was already a bottle of chilled champagne on the table with some warm garlic bread and spiced shrimp in olive oil sauce. Blake's parents and Preach were so amazed that the shrimp were really hot, as if they knew exactly what time the group would walk into the restaurant. Blake introduced everyone to Tiffany and to Blake's delight; they all got along as if they knew each other for years. Tiffany was the type of woman who could talk about everything from politics, finance, sports, fashion or where to find the best bra in town. Blake's parents and Preach fell in love with her instantly. They ate, talked and laughed for three hours.

CHAPTER 7

A Surprised Re-union

Preach excused himself from the group and returned about five minutes later. "Blake, may I see you for a second?" asked Preach. Blake got up from the table and followed Preach to the other part of the restaurant. "What's up dude?" asked Blake. "I want to show you something," said Preach. Blake thought Preach was taking him to the restroom, but as they turned the corner, Preach took Blake to a table of maybe 30 people celebrating someone's birthday. Blake was so busy looking at all the other tables; he didn't notice that Preach was walking straight toward Ricco. Apparently, Ricco was there with his family celebrating his birthday. As Preach and Blake approached the table, Blake finally noticed Ricco at the head of the table, however, to the right of Ricco was a young beautiful familiar face. Blake did his best not to stare, but everything inside him was going completely crazy. "Could it be? No… it can't be…" Blake said to himself.

"Hey Ricco, you remember my nephew Blake?" said Preach. Ricco stood up and shook Blake's hand. "Hey nephew, welcome to our celebration. This is my family and this lovely lady right here is my wife Brandi," said Ricco. Brandi was having the same thoughts as Blake when Ricco introduced her to Blake and Preach. "Pleasure to meet you guys" said Brandi. Brandi, like Blake did her best not to stare and act casual, but inside, she was so surprised stunned and happy to see Blake after all these years. "This looks like a birthday celebration for someone" said Blake. "Yes, it's my birthday today," said Ricco. "Oh wow, I wish we could stay and help you celebrate, but we are on the other side of the restaurant celebrating Blake's engagement to his fiancé" said Preach. Brandi and Blake's eyes locked into each other for a split second. "I saw you from the other side of the room so I thought we would come over and say hello. Nice meeting you all, we'll let you get back to your party, take care" said Preach. At this point Blake couldn't utter a word, his mind was gone. As they got far away from the table where no one could hear them, Preach said," what the f… is wrong with you dude? "That's her!!" said an excited Blake. "That's who?" asked Preach. "That's the girl I told you about when I was in college – she was the one who blew my mind" said Blake. "Oh, okay, that's why your dumb ass was standing there looking stupid!" exclaimed Preach.

"Dude, I was stuck; my brain was jumping through hoops. Damn, and did you see how good she looked?" "Well, she is married to a big time drug dealer who is also a doctor" said Preach. "Do you think she knows he is a big time drug dealer? The person I met in college would never have been involved with a person like that" said Blake. "Blake -trust me, when I tell you this, there are many things in this world that would shock the hell out of some people, so never be surprised by anything, and next time, try harder to not show any reaction in that type of situation!" said Preach. "I didn't react when I saw her" said Blake.

"Dude, the tension that you both created in three seconds was unbelievable. I didn't know what was going on, but I knew something was going on between you two. I just hope he didn't notice anything. Blake, he is not the type of man we need to have problems with, you feel me?" asked Preach. "I understand" said Blake. Preach knew this was going to be a problem for Blake. He knew his nephew very well, but he hoped for everyone's sake that Blake would let it go, especially, since he just got engaged to a beautiful young lady.

On the way home, Tiffany could sense that something was bothering Blake. Blake was always bubbly - full of laughter and much conversation, but this particular night, Blake was totally quiet – his silence was deafening. Tiffany was trying to figure out what on earth could Preach have said to him that could change his mood so drastically. When Blake and Tiffany arrived home, Tiffany immediately took a shower and slipped on some sexy lingerie, figuring this could snap Blake out of the melancholy mood he had suddenly found himself in.

To her surprise, Blake showered and went downstairs and got on his computer. Tiffany tried waiting for him but eventually fell asleep. When she woke, she realized that Blake never came to bed. Tiffany found him asleep on the family room sofa. There was no TV downstairs and not too much furniture, because Tiffany was still in the process of decorating the house. More now than ever, she knew something was wrong and was determined to find out. Tiffany woke Blake up from the sofa and told him they need to talk. In his heart, he knew that his actions last night made Tiffany suspicious. Blake told her they could talk after he got off work later that day. Blake needed time to decide on what he was going to tell Tiffany about his mood swing last night. The moment Blake got to work; he called Preach and asked him whether he knew that Ricco's wife was the girl he was crazy about in college.

"Preach, tell me the truth, did you know that Brandi was the same girl I told you about when I was in college?" asked Blake. "No, I didn't know she was the same girl" said Preach. "Okay, when I was in school and I asked you to find out about Brandi, all you told me was that I should leave her alone and move on. Why did you tell me that?" "At that time, the word I got was that a major player in the drug world was taking care of her and her family and to stay away from that situation; that's why I told you to leave her alone" said Preach. "I didn't know who the person was at the time. Remember, I was trying to move up the food chain in terms of my drug connection during those years, and because of you, I was able to connect with the top guy. I would have never thought it would be Ricco because he is so much older than her" said Preach. "Preach, I can't seem to get her off my mind. All through the night I had thoughts of her.

I couldn't even be with Tiffany from thinking about Brandi so much" said Blake. "Well young fella, you better snap out of it and re-focus on your new fiancé. Remember, Ricco has enough juice to make us disappear. So nephew, for both our sakes, let it go, marry Tiffany and be happy. Tiffany is a gorgeous, smart and wonderful person, don't let an old memory destroy what took you so long to find. This is the first time in my life that I've heard you commit your love to a woman. From what I saw yesterday at dinner, you made a wonderful choice. I've been around a lot longer than you have nephew, girls like Tiffany are hard to find and when you get one, hold on tight and thank God for sending her your way," said Preach. "I hear you sir," said Blake. When Blake got home, Tiffany was there patiently waiting. "Hello dear," said Tiffany as Blake walked in. Tiffany was sipping on a glass of wine and had drunk half the bottle. She was really nervous because up to this point, Blake had always been so calm and smooth regardless of the situation. "I know you're wondering what happened to me last night after we left the restaurant. There was a gentleman on the other side of the restaurant that my uncle Preach is dealing with in the drug game. We found out last night that this dude is much more dangerous than originally anticipated. I'm really worried about my uncle's safety dealing with this guy. That's what was on my mind last night driving home. I apologize for being so quiet in the car, but I was trying to figure out a way for my uncle to continue his livelihood without dealing with that individual. I don't like having these types of conversations with you or even being that close to the situation myself" said Blake. "I understand, but next time; just tell me what's going on instead of having me go crazy with all types of bad thoughts" said Tiffany. "Will do dear" said Blake. "One more thing, please be honest with me no matter how crazy or ugly the situation may be. I can handle what I know. I will not tolerate lying or feeling like I can't trust you. I've been down that road before and I refuse to travel it again," said Tiffany. "I understand and I got you. However, sometimes you have to trust me and know that I will always do what's best for us. I'm not used to sharing my thoughts with anyone, so this may take a little time for me to adjust" said Blake. "I understand, but remember, I'm your partner now, not your buddy on the street" said Tiffany. "Got it" said Blake.

Blake was feeling really guilty about that conversation, because he knew he didn't totally come clean with Tiffany about the restaurant scene. "'Risk vs. Reward' what do you do?" There was a big part of Blake that hoped he could forget about seeing Brandi after all this time. However, he kept wondering how could the girl he met and fell so hard for in college end up with one of the biggest drug dealers on the east coast. A few weeks later, Blake received a call from Preach – "Nephew, we need to talk." "Talk about what? It sounds bad" said Blake. "Trust me, it's very serious, can you meet me at my crib today when you get off work?" asked Preach.

"What's up Preach? You making me think I did something wrong- Is everything okay?" asked Blake. "No, everything is not okay so stop asking me questions and meet me tonight so we can talk" said

Preach. "Okay, I'll be there around 7:00 pm" said Blake. When Blake arrived he saw something he hadn't seen from Preach, he saw fear and concern. "What's up?" asked Blake. "Two weeks ago we saw Ricco at the restaurant celebrating his birthday and he introduced us to his wife Brandi, well apparently, Ricco figured out something was up between you two. If you recall, you and her both acted like you didn't know each other and it was your first time meeting. Well nephew that shit didn't work! I got a call from Ricco last night and he asked me where you went to school, so you know I'm thinking oh shit, Ricco is trying to figure out what's up with you and his wife" said Preach. "Preach, Florida State has over ten thousand students, so it's very possible for me not to know her," said Blake. "Nephew, Stevie Wonder could see the intense vibe that happened between you two that night, so stop saying stupid shit and help me figure this thing out before it gets crazy! Blake, remember Ricco is a smart educated brother just like you, so I need you to start thinking about what his next move would be to find out what's going on with you and her. By the way, I told him you went to South Carolina State to try and shut down that conversation" said Preach. "Preach, why would you lie about that, he can easily have that information verified" said Blake. "Look, mother fucker...like I said, he caught me off guard with the whole conversation and I was trying to think quickly to make it go away," said Preach. "Shit, all he has to do is contact the enrolment office of both schools and he will know I went to Florida State with Brandi. After all this time, what difference does any of this make?" asked Blake. "Well, if the two of you would have been cool and acknowledged that you guys went to the same college it probably wouldn't be a problem, but both of you tried to act like you didn't know each other and now everything is messed up. Blake, think about it from his perspective, why would you and her lie about knowing each other unless there was something about you two that you both do not want to surface. You told me that you never fucked her right? Right? asked Preach. "Preach, trust me, I never hit it." "Did you do anything with her, because if you didn't, I don't understand why both of you would act so funny when you met again. I must be missing something or you're not coming clean about everything, which is it?" asked Preach. "I was totally honest with you; I did not hit her, but we did kiss on one occasion - the day she graduated. After the kiss, I walked away and I never saw her again until the other night; I swear Preach," said Blake. "Well nephew, Ricco is thinking something and everything I have in place is now in jeopardy. Not only is he my connection; but young blood, this dude has enough juice to make both of us disappear," said Preach. "I don't understand what could happen to make him start asking questions about me" said Blake. "Tell you what, you better find out and quick. I found out that his wife works for a big engineering firm downtown, called ITT. I suggest you get in touch with her quietly and find out what the fuck is going on," said Preach. "I'm on it," said Blake.

The next morning while at work, Blake found out the location of Brandi's firm and went there on his lunch break. He went to the lobby of the building and asked the front desk attendant if he could use the phone to call someone upstairs. Blake called Brandi's firm and the receptionist transferred the call to Brandi. "Hello", said Brandi. "Hello Brandi, its Blake. I'm downstairs in your lobby and I really need to speak with you for a moment". "Okay, I'm on my way down," said Brandi. A few moments later, Brandi came from the elevator and walked over to Blake. As Brandi approached Blake, their eyes locked, and both could tell what the other one was thinking and feeling just from that glance. "We can't talk here, too many people in this building know my husband" said Brandi. "My car is next door in the garage, does that work for you?" asked Blake. "Yes, that's much better," said Brandi. When they arrived at Blake's car, Blake opened the door for her to enter and then got himself in. "Let me just say; I'm so sorry if I've caused you any problems. I didn't mean to look at you the way I did at the restaurant," said Brandi. "What?" asked Blake. "I was so surprised to see you that my mind went crazy; I actually forgot that I was with my husband and the family when I looked at you," said Brandi. Blake just stared at Brandi in amazement at what she was telling him. "All these years, I thought I was the only one carrying a torch, I can't believe what I'm hearing," said Blake. "It's true, I've carried you in my spirit since the last time I saw you in college and we kissed," said Brandi. "OMG, I've carried you in my heart since the day I met you on the bench," said Blake. "Really? I can't believe that with all the girls you had back in school," said Brandi. "Brandi, I never believed in love at first sight, but I get it now. I fell hard for you the moment I saw you and after the kiss, I was totally gone, that's why I walked away. I've always been the type of person, who would control his emotions, feelings or whatever you want to call it, but with you, I felt weak and vulnerable and it scared me. I knew you were leaving school, so I thought I would never see you again, but you remained in my heart and my mind. Every girl I met I compared with you but none measured up. You became my dream girl that got away and then like a miracle you showed up in the restaurant and all those old feelings came right back as if they never left", said Blake. "Wow! The moment we left the restaurant and got in the car, my husband started asking me why I was staring at you so hard when he introduced me to you. I didn't know what to say and he could tell that something was off. He knew right away I was not being honest with him and when I got home that night he asked me again to tell him the truth. I told him that you reminded me of someone I once knew back in school," said Brandi.

"Well I'm here to tell you that he didn't buy your answer, he called my uncle Preach and asked him what school I attended," said Blake. "Really?" asked Brandi. "Yes and my uncle lied and told him I went to South Carolina State. You and I both know how easy it would be for him to find out my uncle lied about the school, and then he is going to try to figure out why you both lied to him," said Blake. "He is extremely jealous when it comes to me, sometimes I think he is obsessed and I don't know why," said Brandi. "Brandi, I have to ask you a couple questions, are you in love with your husband?" asked Blake. "I love him but I don't think I've ever been in love with anyone except you, which is crazy within itself. How can I fall in love with someone after one brief encounter?" asked Brandi "I'm trying to understand what happened to the girl I met in school," said Blake. "What do you mean? I'm the same person," said Brandi. "The girl I met in school would have never married a man like that," said Blake. "Am I missing something, he is a nice looking successful dentist that treats me like a queen and always has since I was in college," said Brandi. "My second question is - do you know what your husband does outside of his dental practice?" "What do you mean?" asked Brandi. "Never mind," said Blake. "I have a question for you" said Brandi. "How do you know my husband?" "He is a friend of my uncle, I met him at a party," said Blake. "Your uncle doesn't seem like the type of man that would know my husband," said Brandi. At this point, Blake realized that Brandi had no idea that she got married to a big time drug dealer. "Brandi; based on what my uncle told me, your husband is not letting this go. He is determined to know what's up between you and I, which would be bad for everyone," said Blake. "I truly believe that he can feel my emotions when he mentions your name," said Brandi.

"Do you still have strong feelings for me?" asked Blake. "I'm married now, so there is no need to go down that road. I'm sure you have someone special in your life, I don't see a wedding ring on your finger, so I guess you are not married yet," said Brandi. "I need to know, please tell me" said Blake. "Blake, what I feel for you I have never felt for my husband. It seems like our timing is always off or it's not meant to be," said Brandi. "What if it is meant to be and that's why we keep meeting each other at strange moments in our lives," said Blake. "If it were meant to be we would be together," said Brandi. "Actually, we have been together spiritually for years which is stronger than anything on this planet. Your heart has been with me and my heart has been with you, the funny part is, we didn't know it. He has you physically, but you carried me in your spirit. Brandi, because of what I feel for you I have to let you know who you are married to," said Blake. "What does that mean?" asked Brandi. "You were right when you said my uncle does not seem like the type of man your husband would associate with; that's because my uncle is a major drug dealer in this area and has been all his life", said Blake. "So how and why would my husband be associated with this type of person?" asked Brandi. "I'll give you one guess," said Blake with a heavy heart. "What are you trying to tell me?" asked Brandi. "Your husband is one of the biggest drug dealers in the city and has been for quite some time. My uncle Preach has been getting cocaine from one of his lower level dudes for the past five years, now Preach deals directly with your husband. I met your husband at a meeting with all of his distributors and my uncle took me to the meeting with the hopes of cutting out the middle man between himself and your husband. That was part of the look I was giving you in the restaurant. The Brandi I met in college would NEVER be with this type of dude. "Blake, I'm in total shock right now, I can't believe what you're saying to be true. Ricco has a very successful dental practice. That's why we are able to live in a gated community with million dollar homes and take lavish trips. He buys me the most expensive exquisite gifts. Our life has been so good, he convinced me not to have kids and now you're telling me that my whole world as I know it is a lie! I am not a naïve woman, there is no way this has been going on for all these years and I not know about it. You are making me feel so stupid right now. Blake, there is no way this is true, you must have the wrong person, this can't be true, it just can't."

"I understand that you're having a hard time believing me, but Brandi, just think for a second, how would someone like my uncle know your husband? My uncle is a street dude, which I'm sure you could tell; that's why you were trying to figure out how they knew each other. Furthermore, as I said, I met your husband at a meeting he held for all the people who sold drugs for him," said Blake. Blake could see that Brandi was physically shaken by this news. Blake totally felt her pain as he gave her the bad news. "What do I do now?" asked Brandi. "You pay attention to what's going on concerning him. I'm sure there have been many clues that will shed even more light on what's going on with your husband, - you just have not focused on them yet" said Blake. "Clues like what?" asked Brandi. "Clues like his cell phone rings often and he would either not take the call or he would answer and walk out of the room so no one hears the conversation," said Blake. "He always answered and walked to another room claiming it's a patient," said Brandi. "Your husband has the perfect cover for his lifestyle. Based on your lifestyle, does he have the amount of patients that would support the way you live, just think about it?" asked Blake. "If this is true, you have just turned my world upside down, OMG", said Brandi. "Brandi, I'm not trying to tell you what to do, I just don't want you to get hurt in any way. You mean more to me than you would ever know. I know who your husband is, but I also know what he is capable of just based on what my uncle has shared with me. I do my best to stay away from that world, that's why I was in shock to find out you were married to a drug dealer. All I was thinking after I left the restaurant that night; was "not Brandi, it can't be". "Trust me Blake; I'm not the type of woman that would ever be with a drug dealer. If I find out that what you are saying is true, I'm going to have real problems on my hands," said Brandi. "I agree with you, however, you can never let him know we had this conversation or my life and possibly that of my uncle's will be in jeopardy. I really need you to understand what I'm telling you because lives depend on it," said Blake. "I understand you are telling me that I've been living with a dangerous drug dealer for years without knowing it. Do you have any idea of how stupid I feel right now if what you're saying is true, not to mention the danger that comes with that life?" said Brandi. "If you were someone else, you and I would never have this conversation. I'm telling you this because I realized that you are still in my heart and mind. I feel like it's my responsibility to protect you, which I'm not sure how I will accomplish that task," said Blake. "Do you really feel that way about me?" asked Brandi. "Yes I do," said Blake. "Wow! That means a lot to me," said Brandi. "At this point, I'm not sure what you're going to do, but please remember Ricco cannot know we had this conversation," said Blake. "I got you, I promise that I won't say a word, but I have to figure out what's going on with my husband. I have to get back to work, can I have a number for you if I need to talk?" asked Brandi. Blake provided Brandi with his beeper and office numbers and Brandi went back to work totally frazzled from the conversation with Blake.

Once Blake got back to his desk he called Preach to give him an update on the conversation with Brandi. Blake told Preach everything that was talked about with Brandi and Preach went off on Blake for telling Brandi about Ricco being a drug dealer. Preach told Blake that if Ricco found out he told his wife what's really going on, there would be problems for them both. Blake assured Preach that Brandi gave him her word that she wouldn't say anything. Preach was not as trusting in Brandi as Blake was with this secret. As

Preach explained to Blake, "If Brandi found out the truth and decides to leave him, Ricco would lose his mind and he would figure out someone dropped a dime on him; not to mention that my connection may be gone, which is major for me," said Preach.

Over the next several weeks, Brandi paid close attention to things at home that were pretty obvious after the conversation with Blake. Brandi knew Ricco had a safe in his house but never really thought about why. Why does Ricco have a safe in the house, why not keep your cash in the bank like every legitimate dentist? She also realized that she didn't have the combination to the safe. In fact, Ricco had never opened the safe in her presence. As Brandi started to reflect on their previous vacations, she thought about the fact that Ricco always paid for everything in cash. He would take $9K in cash on every trip they took. He played it off by telling her that he doesn't like debt and if you pay cash, you can afford the thing that you're doing. She also thought about Ricco weekend trips to Florida every three months. He always said they were conferences, but what conferences are held over the weekend. Suddenly, everything was starting to make sense. Brandi knew if she did a little investigating, she would know for sure, but there was a big part of her that was afraid to know the truth. However, the more she starting thinking about the habits of her husband, she was pretty sure everything Blake said was true, and if so, now what?

After the encounter with Brandi, Blake's entire demeanor with Tiffany had changed. He wasn't as attentive, passionate and talkative; basically, Blake was not himself anymore. He was worried about Brandi's safety, his uncle's business and his own safety if Brandi reneged on her word and told Ricco what they spoke about. Tiffany noticed Blake had become a little distant but she thought it was wedding jitters that all men went through, so she didn't think it was something that should cause over-reaction. Tiffany went on with planning the wedding and tried to give Blake some space with the wedding plans unless it was necessary.

While Tiffany was out shopping for the house one evening, she thought it would be good to include Blake for the decoration of the theatre room in his house. She asked Blake to meet her at "Elite HTS" the most popular home theatre store in the DC area. Blake and Tiffany picked out theatre furniture and accessories for the room. While they were shopping, Blake was reminded why he fell in love with Tiffany in the first place. Tiffany was truly Blake's equal. Tiffany was smart, gorgeous, sexy and funny as hell, just like Blake when he is his normal self. The stress that Blake had been feeling for the past weeks, suddenly went away; once he focused on Tiffany and everything she brought to the table.

After shopping, Tiffany and Blake went to Legal Seafood Restaurant in the area and ate, drank and had a great time. For the first in a long time, Blake became himself again. Later that night, he and Tiffany made love like there was no tomorrow. Their relationship was finally back to normal and Blake was at peace, he was in a happy place again - at least for the moment. Blake was so happy, he even agreed to a wedding date proposed by Tiffany. The wedding was scheduled to take place in six months. Tiffany, her mom and Blake's mom, became super busy getting the wedding details in place while Blake focused on being happy and getting Brandi out of his system once again.

This happiness was however short-lived for Blake as one morning Brandi called telling him they needed to talk. When a woman tells a man "we need to talk" it's NEVER something men want to hear. Blake agreed to meet Brandi on his lunch hour in the parking garage of her building, where they last spoke. Blake dreaded hearing what Brandi was about to say, because somehow, he knew it wouldn't be good news for him or his uncle Preach. As Brandi entered Blake's car, Blake could feel the tension of emotion and the look on her face said it all. "You confirmed it didn't you?" asked Blake. "You were right about EVERYTHING, I mean EVERYTHING!!" said

RISK vs. REWARD

Brandi as she began to cry. "How did you confirm it was true?" asked Blake. "All I had to do was pay attention, the signs were everywhere and to make matters worse; I found out that he had been cheating on me for years," said a heavily crying Brandi. Blake held her in his arms and did his best to comfort her. "Brandi, I'm so sorry, but you know women come with the territory of being a drug dealer. "I know it does, that's why I've always told myself that I would never date or deal with a drug dealer for that reason and the risk factor that comes with that life. Blake; isn't that the reason we went to college and got our degrees, so we would not deal with people in that world and create a safe environment for our families?" "I feel like such a fool right now, this man has played me for our entire marriage. I wanted you to meet me today to let you know that I confronted him last night about all of this shit." "You did what?"

"How did you confront him?" asked Blake. "Well, after doing some research, I found out that he has a complete family down in Florida, that's part of the reason he goes there every three months. He has been seeing this lady for the past five years and they have a three year old son together. He also has a daughter with another woman in Florida, this kid is also three years old; and for the cherry on top, he has a set of 10 month old twins by another woman here in DC. This dude has been spreading his penis all over the fucking

East Coast. I obtained documentary evidence of all the kids, his name is on all the birth certificates as the father and I also contacted the women and they all think he is their man exclusively - can you believe that shit? When I confronted him last night, he acted like it was no big deal. Remember that scene from the movie "Enough" when Jennifer Lopez confronted her husband for cheating and he slapped the shit out of her? Well, the same thing happened to me last night, Ricco slapped the shit out of me for telling him I know about him cheating and that he is a drug dealer.

"He also told me that I better not think about leaving him; and if I did, he would make sure I'm six feet under and no one would find me. I could tell from the look in his eyes that he meant every word. What the f.... have I gotten myself into?"

"At this point, I don't know what to do Blake. I can't go on living with Ricco, but if I try to leave, he will kill me. "Brandi, unfortunately, I don't have answers for you right now. I do know, somehow, someway, you need to get away from this man, I just don't know how right now, but you and I are smart enough to figure it out without someone dying.

After the situation with Brandi calmed down somewhat, Ricco decided to have someone watch Brandi, because he knew someone was feeding her information and was determined to find out where it was coming from. Ricco saw the fear and hurt in her eyes and wasn't sure what she would do. However, Ricco knew Brandi was smart enough to hurt him in the worst way possible and to change the situation - this is what he feared the most. The thought of losing her was more than he could bear. Ricco knew he had a dynamite woman in Brandi. Brandi was a man's dream, super smart, gorgeous body and face, with the most down to earth spirit that is rare to find from a woman that looked like her.

Brandi was a highly spiritual person, which Ricco figured would be the biggest problem in this entire situation. Ricco did not attend church, but Brandi was a devoted member who also taught bible study sessions on Tuesdays. Ricco knew that Brandi's heart would never allow her to deal with everything she had recently discovered about him; but, his ego would not let her just walk away from him. The million dollar question was - could he convince her to stay and secondly, what was he willing to do to make it happen; Risk vs. Reward.

CHAPTER 8

The Grand Plan

After talking with Brandi, Blake met with Preach to provide him another update. During the conversation with Blake and Preach, Preach went off on Blake for telling Brandi about Ricco's drug business. "Nephew, why the fuck would you tell that female about Ricco's side hustle? Don't you know that most women can't hold water?! You do understand that if she shared with Ricco that the information came from you we will most definitely have a war on our hands? Do you understand what I'm saying to you?" "I understand Preach, but Brandi assured me that she didn't mention my name to Ricco". "And you believe that, even after he slapped her around, you think she still held your secret?" "I hope you're right nephew, if not, everything will get ugly real fast, said Preach." "I have to figure out a way to get her away from Ricco and I need your wisdom on how to do it, said Blake." "Okay nephew, the three of us need to talk, so tell you what. Call her and tell her to meet us outside the city to make sure we are not seen by anyone because this cannot get back to Ricco. Blake called Brandi and they agreed to meet in Richmond at the King's Dominion parking lot. Unbeknownst to the three, Brandi was being followed by Ricco's henchman. After the three arrived at the parking lot, Brandi left her car in the parking lot and got in Preach's SUV and headed to the Marriott hotel. Preach's SUV windows were tinted so the henchman couldn't see who was actually in the car.

As they pulled into the parking lot of the Marriott and got out of the car, only Brandi and Blake exited the vehicle. Preach stayed in the car to make a phone call. Blake went to the front desk and checked in while Brandi sat in the lobby. The henchman pulled up in front of the hotel and could see both Brandi and Blake. It appeared to him as though they were getting a room, which was what they did.

The henchman left the hotel to report to Ricco. Blake and Brandi went to the room as they waited for Preach. The henchman called Ricco and told him that Preach brought his nephew Blake down there to meet with Brandi and that he dropped them off at a hotel. He also told Ricco that Preach left after dropping them off. Ricco automatically thought Brandi was on revenge sex with Blake because of the information she now has on him. Ricco was furious and told the henchman to return to the city right away. During the time Brandi was with Blake alone, they talked about how bad the situation was and how to get everyone out of harm's way without causing major hardship for everyone. Brandi also made it clear to Blake that she wanted to maintain her lifestyle she became accustomed to.

By this time, Preach was knocking at the hotel room door, Blake let him in. "Hello Brandi, nice to meet you again. I just have one question for you both. Why do people with college degrees make the dumbest life decisions when a little heat comes their way? You and my nephew lied about knowing each other which was stupid as shit and then my dumb ass nephew told you about your husband being a drug dealer, which is something you should have figured out a long time ago, and both of you have college degrees - really!!!! Let me just say this, in order for you to get away from Ricco, you will have to leave this city. There is no way in hell you can walk away from here and think you can live in the same city. DC is a very small place where everyone knows everyone and one day he will find you, trust me on that one. Do you have family in other cities or is there somewhere you would like to live?" asked Preach. I have an aunt in Dallas and my company's corporate office is there, said Brandi." "Has Ricco even gone to Dallas with you to visit your aunt? asked Preach. "No," said Brandi. "Brandi, I have to ask you this question and I need total honesty from you. Did you tell Ricco that Blake told you about his side hustle? "No," said Brandi. "Let me be perfectly clear to both of you, if Ricco thinks Blake or I was involved in you knowing what you know, it would be world war 3 on the streets. He would put a hit on both of us, so I need both of you to know how serious this really is for all three of us," said Preach. "Uncle, we understand, we know the severity of the situation," said Blake. "So for now Brandi, you have to act like everything is okay and start working on a job relocation very discreetly at work. Once you get a date, let Blake know and we will figure the next step from there," said Preach.

Everyone agreed with the plan and they headed back to Brandi's car to have her dropped off. Meanwhile, Ricco was planning his next move against Preach and Blake. Ricco, went over his books to figure out how much money Preach owed him. Normally, Ricco would "front" Preach 30 kilos of cocaine at $20K per kilo and Preach would pay him within 2 months. Ricco and Preach had established a great relationship once Preach was able to cut out the middle man, to the point where Ricco lowered his price even more for Preach. Ricco knew that even though he lowered the price for Preach, he would still make just as much money due to Preach's ability to sell the dope so quickly.

Two days later, Preach received a phone call from Ricco, Preach knew right away that something was wrong because Ricco NEVER called Preach. Preach would call Ricco when he was done selling the product to re-up. They had a code and an understanding between the two. When Preach called Ricco, he only said one word "DONE". Ricco's response would be "tomorrow at noon." Preach knew Ricco would meet him at their location tomorrow at noon to get his new package. Their meeting place was always on 295 high-way near Boiling AFB. That location was best for spotting the police which would give them time to get rid of the merchandise if ever necessary. Most drug deals would not take place in a closed area where the police could box the dealer into a corner or trap him into a location. Meeting on the highway is the way Ricco stayed out of harm's way without cops catching him or his crew red handed. Preach didn't answer Ricco's call but listened to the voice message that he left on the answering service. "Yo Preach, I need that cheese by Friday noon," said Ricco. Preach knew from that voicemail that Ricco was up to something. His debt with Ricco was $600K and was due to him in less than a week. That was a clear indication that he was being cut off after this payment was made. Preach called Blake immediately

RISK vs. REWARD

"Nephew, we need to talk as soon as possible, meet me at my house at 6:00 pm." Blake had a bad feeling about that phone call. He arrived at Preach's crib ten minutes before six. His gut feeling told him that something was about to go down. Preach explained to Blake his business dealings with Ricco. Afterwards, Blake gave Preach his assessment of the situation. "I think Ricco is looking to hurt you, me and Brandi. The fact that he is asking you for money that is normally due in a couple months is a clear indication you are being squeezed out of the game. My only question is - do you think it will stop there? My impression of Ricco is he will stop at nothing to get what he wants, and right now, he wants me, you and Brandi to suffer. I'm just not sure what degree of suffering he has in mind," said Blake. "I hear you nephew and I think you're on point with your thoughts. My big problem right now is that I will not have the $600K by Friday. I just put 50% of the product on the street, and I'm not going to squeeze my good soldiers because dude is on his period over his wife" said Preach. "How much are you short?" asked Blake. "$200K," said Preach. "What is your plan to get it by Friday?" asked Blake. "There is no plan, I don't have a source from which to get that type of cash. The people who have that type of cash are my competitors and they would love to see me out of business," said Preach. "Let me ask you a question, if you pay him and he cuts you off, what is the plan going forward?" asked Blake. "Not sure right now, everything is coming at me too fast to think straight right now. My immediate thought right now is, what if I don't pay him all his money by Friday, let's talk about that situation. Nephew, if for any reason Ricco thinks or knows you fucked his wife, he would put a hit out on you and me. I need you to understand that's who we are dealing with", said Preach. "I understand, give me some time to think of a plan and I will get back to you by tomorrow," said Blake.

When Blake arrived home, Tiffany was there with dinner, and champagne. Even though Blake's world had been turned upside down, Tiffany was in fiancé bliss. She was floating on cloud nine knowing she was marrying the man of her dreams. Blake did his best to hide what was going on outside their relationship. However, Tiffany was so tuned into Blake, she could sense when something wasn't right. Blake and Tiffany ate dinner talked a little and headed to bed. Blake was always a very loving type of man in the bed, but this night, because of what was on his mind, he was not his usual self and Tiffany knew it. Tiffany thought back to the night they announced their engagement to Blake's parents and how strange Blake was acting the rest of that evening. In Tiffany's eyes, the exact type of strangeness from Blake was happening again, which made her deeply concerned. Tiffany was a very smart young lady and she felt like she really knew her man, now at this moment she was starting to question her own judgment of Blake. Up to this point Tiffany felt like they shared a very open and honest relationship. Now, all this was in question, with his repeated mysterious behavior. At this point, Tiffany's mind was made up about finding out what the fuck was going on with her man.

The next morning Blake went to work with the worries of the world on his shoulders. In the back of his mind, he felt like all the drama that he, Preach and Brandi were facing was because of him not keeping his mouth shut to Brandi about her husband. As a result, while Blake was in his office, he came up with a plan to get Preach the money he needed. Blake and Preach knew that if Ricco didn't get his $600K by Friday, their lives could possibly be over. As the Financial Analyst, Blake figured out a way to get the funds from Georgetown and put it back before anyone would know. Blake changed the wire instructions for one of the investments firms the University had in its portfolio to his cousin Gary's account. As long as the money was returned before the end of month, the accounting department would not have problems during their monthly reconciliation. Once the transaction was completed, Blake walked outside his office building to call Preach from his cell phone and let him know that he had the money. "Hey Preach!" "What's up nephew?" asked Preach. "We need to meet up later tonight to discuss some things, I have the funds you need" said Blake. "Nephew, don't play me like that, this shit is serious!" said Preach. "No joke Preach, straight up," said Blake. "Can we meet you at your new house later, since I haven't seen it yet?" asked Preach. "Sure, let's meet up at 9", said Blake. "Cool, I'm out," said Preach. Blake then made a call to his cousin Gary and asked him to meet him at his house at 9:00 pm.

Unbeknownst to Blake, Tiffany had not gone to work that day. She wanted to come up with a plan that could give her clues as to what was going on with Blake. Tiffany met up with her sister to talk through her thoughts about what she was feeling. The two sisters figured out he was either cheating or lied about being in the drug game and shit was going bad. The sisters went and spoke to a private investigator and received some tips on how to find out things on your own. One of the suggestions was for Tiffany to purchase four small tape recorders and place them in rooms in which her fiancé spent a lot of time by himself.

Tiffany took his advice because this was much cheaper than hiring a private investigator. Tiffany went back to the house and placed the tape recorders in areas where Blake spent most of his time. The PI had instructed her to place it in such a way that it would be easy for her to press the record button without his knowledge when he is in a room.

Tiffany followed the instructions and waited for Blake to come home, hoping to learn what was causing these major mood swings. Blake came home being his normal loving self towards Tiffany, which really through her for a hoop, considering last night and this morning, everyone could tell that the weight of the world was on his shoulders. Now, the Blake she met and came to love walked through the door. Blake gave Tiffany one of those kisses that said, can we get it in real quick before dinner; and that's what happened. Blake gave it to Tiffany like he did when they first met. Tiffany was extremely happy and more confused now than ever. She actually started to second guess her feelings, funny how good sex can do that to a woman.

Later that evening, the doorbell rang and Tiffany answered, "Hey Gary," said Tiffany. "Hey Tiffany, long time no see. I saw your sister a couple weeks ago and she told me about the house," said Gary. "When are you going to settle down, and love just one woman?" asked Tiffany. They both laughed right after she finished that sentence. "You got jokes girl!" where is my boy?" asked Gary. "He is in the family room watching the game. My bad, go straight ahead and make a right," said Tiffany with much laughter. As Gary walked away, Tiffany yelled at him "You ain't gonna change, I feel sorry for any woman who think they will calm you down." A couple minutes later the doorbell rang again and Tiffany answered, "Hey Preach." "Hey baby girl, what's happening? Are you enjoying this fabulous new house with my nephew?" asked Preach.

"Absolutely! Let me take you to the men around the corner," said Tiffany. Tiffany walked Preach into the room where Blake and Gary were drinking Moet. After the men embraced and acknowledge each other, Tiffany told the men she would excuse herself so they could talk. As Tiffany left the room, she was able to press the record button under the sofa Preach was about to sit on by dropping her napkin in her hand on the floor on her way out.

Blake explained to Preach and Gary that he got the $200K needed for Ricco. He also informed Gary that the funds were wired into his bank account and that the money has to be replaced before the end of the month. Gary and Preach both asked Blake where he got the money, he told them not to worry about that, but he reminded them both several times that the money had to be returned before the end of the month. Preach assured him that he would have the funds by the 25th of the month. At this point the three started discussing what if situations; like Ricco wanting to kill them after he got his cash. The conversation then turned into a plan to be proactive in this situation. "Maybe we should kill him and keep all the money. We don't know if Ricco will be the one who collects the payment, sometimes, he sends one of his henchmen for those types of transactions. If he really plans on killing us after receiving payment, he definitely would not be there when that goes down. And what about Brandi, how will we protect Brandi in this given situation?" asked Blake. "Nephew, I know you feel some type of way about this chick, but we can only protect ourselves in this given situation," said Preach. "Let me and my boys take him out tomorrow and all the problems will be solved," said Gary. "Getting to him is not that easy," said Preach. "Look, let me think for a day and come up with a plan that will keep me, you and Brandi safe from this dude. In the meantime, the money is sitting in your account Gary so don't touch it until you hear from me and we come up with a plan to make everyone happy and safe," said Blake. "Look here, all three of us need to be coming up with a plan to fix this situation, because right now nephew, your thinking is cloudy because of Brandi," said Preach. "Who is Brandi?" asked Gary "That's a long story that I don't want to go into right now. Let me just say this, it's unfinished business for Blake," said Preach. "What's up cuz?" asked Gary. "Not now," said Blake. "Let's meet tomorrow night at the Grand Hyatt around 7 and try to finalize what we're going to do," said Preach.

"Okay," said Preach. Blake walked Gary and Preach outside to their cars as they kept talking about the situation. They both yelled bye to Tiffany as they walked outside. Tiffany yelled from upstairs, "Bye!"

While the men were outside talking, Tiffany came downstairs and retrieved the tape recorder she had placed in the family room. The next morning on her way to work Tiffany listened to the tape in her car and was devastated with everything she heard. More importantly, she was trying to figure out who was Brandi and why Preach said that was unfinished business for Blake. The thought of Blake cheating on her was totally unacceptable and Tiffany was determined to get to the bottom of what was going on. In her mind, she couldn't make sense of him cheating on her. Blake had been the most attentive, generous and loving man she had encountered. Tiffany knew she hit the jackpot when they hooked up and was not going down without a fight. Tiffany knew Blake loved her with all his heart, so this situation was more than confusing for her than ever. All day at work, Tiffany could only think about who Brandi was and what Blake felt for her. As most women do, Tiffany searched her brain for red flags during their relationship where Blake could have been doing some extra-curricular stuff without her knowledge. She couldn't come up with anything. Blake had been the perfect boyfriend by any woman's standard. Regardless, finding out who Brandi was and protecting her future husband from being killed became her top priority at this point.

Gary, Preach and Blake met later that evening at the Grand Hyatt hotel to discuss the plan to resolve their immediate problem - RICCO. Gary stuck with his plan of letting his crew kill him and be done with it. Preach's idea was to rob him and then kill him. Blake, being the most level headed of the three, actually came up with a plan that was well throughout and practical for the situation. Blake told Preach and Gary of the steps - Brandi has to leave the house on Thursday when Ricco goes to work with the intentions of not returning. Her company's corporate office is located in Dallas Texas and I'm sure she can secure a position there. I'm pretty sure Ricco would never think to look for her in Texas, if it came to that. So Thursday morning, Brandi would take all her clothes to a hotel in Virginia outside the city until her flight to Texas on Saturday. I have a friend from college in Texas that will let her stay with him until she gets her own place. Brandi has quite a bit of money saved up over the years of living with Ricco. "Hell, I guess so, her ass probably hasn't paid a bill in 7 years or so, she should be rich," said Preach with laughter. "Preach, I have a question for you. Where do you normally meet Ricco to give him his money?" asked Blake "Most times we meet on the highway, either 295 or 395, it just depends on what he is doing that day," said Preach. "Okay, see if you can get him to meet you on 295, by Boiling Air Force Base. We will have a nice surprise waiting for him when he arrives," said Blake. "What's the play nephew?" asked Preach. "I'm gonna have someone watching him all morning to make sure we know what he is up to. When it's time for him to meet you, the person watching him will put a slight puncture in one of his tires. He would be able to meet you but, by the time the meeting is through, his tire would be completely flat. Knowing that Ricco wear's nothing but Italian suits, he would gladly welcome someone to help change that tire. That's when my man who was watching him all morning will pull up to help. He will handle Ricco for us?" said Blake. "What do you mean when you say, he will handle Ricco? asked Preach. "Preach, trust me, he has instructions to do exactly what I told him to do. Once it's done, Ricco will be looking at 20 years in jail, if not more," said Blake. "Nephew, what the fuck do you have planned?" asked Preach. "Just trust me uncle, the less people know the better, you taught me that remember?" said Blake. "I trust you nephew, I know your ass is smart, I just hope you covered all the bases and anticipated things not going the way you plan. The best plans have a way of going off track," said

Preach. "I think I'm ready for anything Ricco can come up with," said Blake.

CHAPTER 9

Executing the Plan

Thursday morning, Brandi left the house for work like she normally did. Brandi would leave the house at 7:00 am and Ricco would leave at 8:30 am. Brandi went to a local coffee shop and waited for Ricco to leave the house. What Brandi didn't realize is that she was being followed by one of Ricco's henchmen. The henchman called Ricco to let him know that Brandi was still in the neighborhood at a local coffee shop. Ricco knew something was up, he just didn't know what it was. The henchman told Ricco that Brandi was waiting on something or someone. Ricco told him to follow her all day and report anything unusual. Ricco told his crew that he was meeting up with Preach to get his money and he would let them know what he wanted done after he was paid. Ricco made several calls before he left the house and put some things in place for the day. Ricco finally left the house at 9:00 am and Brandi saw his car drove by while she was in the coffee shop. At that point, she left the coffee shop and headed back to the house. She went inside and started packing her clothes into suitcases and trash bags. The henchman saw her take several trash bags to her car but was confused about what could be inside the bags. After loading her car with bags and two suitcases, Brandi headed out of the neighborhood to the beltway. Brandi drove to the Hilton in Tyson Corner, Virginia. She parked her car in the garage and checked into the hotel. She called Blake and told him she had her clothes and was now in the hotel. The henchman called Ricco and informed him that Brandi drove to the Hilton hotel in VA. Ricco asked the henchman if he saw Blake at the hotel. His response was in the negative. Blake was relieved that Brandi was out of the house and safe in Virginia. Blake thought, so far so good at this point. Gary hooked up that morning with Preach and gave him the $200K needed to pay Ricco. Preach and Ricco had set a time of 1:00 pm to meet on freeway 295. All Ricco could think of was Brandi in the hotel to hook up with Blake, and the thought of that idea drove him crazy.

Ricco called the hotel to confirm that Brandi was there and to find out what room she was staying. Ricco told the hotel operator that it was their 10 year anniversary and that he wanted to send a special gift from the top jewelry store in the area which would require his wife to sign for it. He explained that the gift cost more than $50K and the operator told him she was in room 702. Ricco started to plan a strategy to deal with Brandi and Blake's betrayal. Ricco was so consumed with the idea of Blake sleeping with his wife; he decided to send someone else to get the money from Preach with instructions to kill him after they got the loot. Ricco sent his top henchman to meet with Preach while he decided to go to the hotel and handle the Brandi situation personally. Blake told Preach to be careful at the meeting with Ricco and to make sure he stayed in his car. Blake was very adamant to Preach to not get out of his car, and have Ricco come to his car to get paid. Preach arrived at the meeting location 20 minutes before time to make sure he was not walking into an ambush of any kind. Preach also wanted to place a couple pistols in certain locations in case things went south. As Preach sat there waiting on Ricco, Preach noticed Ricco's Jaguar pulled up, but he couldn't tell who was in the car because of the tinted windows. Normally, when Ricco pulled up, he would get out the car and speak to Preach and make the transaction at Preach's trunk. However, this time would be different because Preach was not picking up product, just making a payment. Preach sat there looking in his rear window waiting for Ricco to call him but he didn't. Preach knew something was not right. Preach called Ricco and there was no answer. At this point Preach grabbed one of the guns and held it in his lap, waiting for Ricco to get out of the car. All on a sudden, a dude got out of Ricco's car and noticed that his rear tire had gone flat. Preach was trying to figure out who was the dude driving Ricco's car and what he was looking at. Preach didn't realize he was looking at the tire when he got out of the car. As the guy was looking at the tire, another SUV pulled up and two dudes got out with guns and attacked the driver who was in Ricco's car.

Preach was watching everything through his rear view mirror trying to figure out what the fuck was going on. Preach's instincts told him to pull off and figure this shit out later. The two dudes knocked the driver out and put him in the trunk of Ricco's car. They also left a package on the floor inside the vehicle. After a few hours, the police noticed the abandoned vehicle on the side of the highway and pulled over to investigate the situation. The cops found the package on the floor inside the vehicle, which turned out to be 2 kilo grams of cocaine. They also noticed that the keys were still in the ignition and took the opportunity to open the trunk and found the man in the trunk with a loaded semi-automatic weapon tucked in his pants. The police realized immediately that something big was going on. The police arrested the dude in the car and charged him for distribution and possession of an illegal firearm.

Those charges carry a minimum sentence of 15 years in prison if convicted. Once the dude was able to make a phone call, he called Ricco and told him what happened. Ricco knew immediately that he was being set up by Preach! Once Preach got to a quiet area, he called Blake to tell him what went down with the drop. "Nephew, something crazy is happening; Ricco didn't show up for the money, someone else showed up that I've never seen before, so I pulled off," said Preach. "What? Preach - please tell me that you're kidding! I had a different plan in place that I didn't tell you about," said Blake. "What plan?" asked Preach. "I had a plan that would keep everyone safe and get Ricco out of the picture for a long time," said Blake. "Why didn't you tell me the plan changed? I could have gotten killed today nephew," said Preach. "Preach we have a real problem now; if Ricco was not in the car, then whoever was driving had probably contacted him by now and told him what happened when you left. If that's the case, Ricco knows we were setting him up to go to jail for a long time," said Blake. "Nephew, what was your damn plan?" asked Preach. "The plan was for the police to catch him with $600K in cash, 2 kilo grams and a gun. The combination of the three will make him go away for at least 30 years, minimum!! But, if you left before making the drop and someone else got jammed up for the charge, Ricco will realize he was being set up. My guys were to get him before anything happened to you, so as you can see Preach, I was looking out for you, me and Brandi. So if Ricco didn't make the pickup, where is he?" asked Blake. "Blake, I know you thought you were looking out for everyone, but that was a dumb ass plan. I told you Ricco may not be in the car because he was planning to kill me. If that was his plan, remember, men like him don't get their hands dirty. I figured he would come with someone else to do the murder once he got his money. For him not to show up at all means that he knew something was up or he didn't care about the money and wanted me dead. That means we are all in danger, especially his wife. Where is she?" I have her at the Hilton, in Tyson Corner, VA.

Preach thoughts rang true; the dude driving Ricco's car was arrested and received his one phone call. He called Ricco and told him everything that happened. Ricco had a suspicion that something was not right when he woke up in the morning. As a result, he had one of his henchmen following Brandi all day to keep tabs on her. As Preach predicted, Ricco plan was to kill him when the money was picked up. However, Ricco was too smart to make the hit himself, so he sent someone else to take care of it. However, after learning what took place with the hit, Ricco now knows for sure that Preach, Blake and Brandi were all in on setting him up to go to jail for a long time. Ricco knew Brandi was at the Hilton hotel, probably waiting on Blake whom he assumed she had been having an affair with behind his back. At this point, it didn't matter; all of them had to die and Ricco was determined to make sure it happened as soon as possible. Ricco called his henchman who followed Brandi to the Hilton hotel to inquire if he had seen Blake with her or whether she was alone. The henchman informed Ricco that she checked into the hotel alone and that he hadn't seen Blake or Preach on the property. Ricco's brain was spinning 100 mph, trying to figure out his next move and what they were up to. One thing for certain, Ricco knew they wanted him out the picture. Ricco called the henchman watching Brandi and told him to pick him up from his office. After the arrest, Ricco's car was impounded by the cops.

After learning what went down with Preach and the payment pickup, Blake called Brandi at the hotel to tell her to lock the door and not open it under any circumstances until she heard back from him. At this point, Brandi was terrified about what was going on. She started asking Blake if everything was okay with their plan or has something gone wrong. Blake didn't want to worry her, so he told her there was a minor snag but everything was still on schedule, which couldn't be farther from the truth. Blake started to think about the plan that was in place, but in light of the recent events, he didn't think he could trust it. Blake knew Ricco was not a dumb man, so he knew he had to think quickly and strategize about a new plan and figure out Ricco's next move against him, Brandi and Preach. Blake called a friend that worked one block from the Hilton and asked him to get a room for him. He told his friend that it was very important to get a room on the second floor, close to the elevator. Blake's friend did it without hesitation, thinking that Blake had a trick he wanted to smash without being spotted. Blake told him to leave the key at the front desk in an envelope with the name "Brandi" on it. Once that was done, Blake called Brandi and told her to go get the envelope from the front desk and move her stuff to the new room on the second floor, but not to let the hotel know what she was doing. Brandi made the room change and confirmed with Blake that she was now in room 206. All of this had Brandi more worried now than ever. Still, Blake reassured her that everything was okay and that he was on his way to the hotel. Blake knew that things were now spinning out of control, and that he needed to act quickly if he wanted to keep himself, Preach and Brandi out of harm's way. Blake left work immediately and called Preach and Gary and told them to meet him at the Hilton by Tyson Corner,

VA, immediately. He also told them to come strapped!!

On the way to the hotel, Blake stopped by a friend's house to get a pistol. At this point, Blake knew he had to be ready for whatever was coming his way.

The entire morning at work Tiffany was consumed with finding out who Brandi was and why Ricco wanted to kill her future husband, Preach and Gary. Tiffany called her sister and asked her if she knew Preach. Her sister told her that she met him a couple times at Gary's place, but didn't know much about him. All she knew was that he always had a lot of money in his pocket whenever he showed up and every time he came over he had a different girl with him. Tiffany's sister said she thought he was a big time drug dealer, but she wasn't 100% sure. Every time Preach came over, he always had a bag in his hand and would go in the bedroom with Gary for 10 minutes or so and come out. Her sister wasn't sure what they were doing or talking about. Tiffany was very hesitant, but eventually made a call to a friend who works for the Drug Enforcement Administration (DEA). "Hey Mike, this is Tiffany, how are you?" "Hey stranger, what's happening?" You know we really miss you here in the office. Have you considered coming back to the agency? You were the best investigator we ever had!" "Mike, you know I still haven't gotten over that incident that happened three years ago," said Tiffany. "I understand, but you know it happens to the best of us and we have to shake it off and keep it moving," said Mike. "That's easier said than done. I used to think about it often but as time went by, it got a little easier to deal with if you know what I mean." said Tiffany. "You know I've been there and done that numerous times, so yes, I know what you mean," said Mike. "I have a personal favor I need to ask you, strictly off the record," said Tiffany. "Off the record, this must be really important for you to call me sounding the way you do," said Mike. "It is," said Tiffany. "What's up?" "Do you know anyone called Ricco that's in the game here in the DC area," asked Tiffany? "There is a big time dentist called Ricco that's in the game we've been investigating for years," said Mike. "Can you provide me some detailed information on him?" asked Tiffany. "Like what?" asked Mike. "You know, the usual breakdown of a suspect," said Tiffany. "How quickly do you need this info," asked Mike "Like yesterday," said Tiffany. "Is your private email still the same, if so, give me 15 minutes," said Mike. "It is. Mike, thanks for not asking too many of questions," said Tiffany. "Tiff, I've known you for too long, you will tell me when the time is right, no worries," said Mike. Fifteen minutes later, Tiffany had a detailed file on Ricco and known associates.

PREACH

After a few minutes of reading, Tiffany headed to a storage unit 10 minutes away from her office. Tiffany went inside her unit and came out with a black duffle bag, and headed to Ricco's dental office. It took Tiffany 30 minutes to arrive at the dental office, once there; she noticed a black Cadillac Escalade SUV with chrome wheels and tinted windows parked right in front of the door with the engine running. She sat there for a moment trying to figure out her next move when a very distinguished looking gentleman who fit the description of Ricco walked out. He got into the passenger seat and the SUV pulled off. Once inside the vehicle, Ricco called another of his henchmen (Black) to meet him at the Hilton hotel in Tyson Corner, VA. Tiffany followed the vehicle thinking about how she should handle the situation without getting herself in legal trouble but making sure nothing happened to Blake.

Meanwhile, Blake arrived at the hotel, parked in the garage next to Brandi's car and took the elevator upstairs to Brandi's room. Gary and Preach called him earlier and told him they would get there within an hour. They both had to make stops to get prepared for whatever was about to go down. Blake told Gary that he was in room 206 and to come straight to the room when they arrived.

Blake knocked on door 206 where Brandi was. "Who is it?" asked Brandi. "It's me Blake." Brandi immediately opened the door and Blake entered the room with a very concerned look on his face. "What's wrong?" asked Brandi. "Everything went wrong with my plan this morning" said Blake. "What do you mean everything?" asked Brandi. "Everything! Blake told Brandi the plan that was in place and how Ricco had someone else driving his car and whoever that person was got arrested for possession of drugs and a weapon charge." Blake explained whoever was in that car had probably called Ricco by now and explained everything that went down. "That's why you had me change rooms in the hotel? asked Brandi. "Yes, I'm not sure if Ricco knows where you are or he may have had someone follow you. He must have known something for him not to have been in that car this morning."

Based on what happened, I'm sure he will be coming after me, you and Preach, so I'm taking no chances. I can't let anything happen to you or Preach. I feel like all of this is my fault. My feelings for you put everyone in this situation," said Blake. "I must admit that I was really shocked to find out you still had feelings for me after all this time. I thought it was just me feeling that way," said Brandi.

The crazy part about all of this is that my feelings for you have grown even stronger since we re-united," said Blake. "I realized you cared deeply for me to tell me that I was married to the biggest drug dealer in the

DC area. You had to know that your life would be in danger by telling me that and yet, you told me anyway. Blake, you became so special to me in one day at college and then you did it again after college. Are we destined to be together or what? We both have this amazing attraction to each other and only acted on it once, for a brief moment. I've thought about that kiss you gave me in college a thousand times," said Brandi. "Really?" asked Blake "Yes, a thousand times yes - for many years, the thought of you consumed me, but I figured you had gone on with your life and some sweet young lady probably erased all memories you had of me," said Brandi. "Wow, I'm flattered and amazed that you carried those feelings for so long. Truth be told, I also was consumed by the thought of you for many years after college. In fact, I just met someone that I finally had feelings for. The night I saw you in the restaurant with Ricco was my engagement night. However, after seeing you, my mind went into shock and disbelief that the girl of my dreams was right before me again. I thought I would never see you again in life.

You have no idea how happy and sad I was to see you again that night. I had you so high on a pedestal that only Jesus could knock you down," said Blake. Brandi and Blake both laughed and at that moment their eyes connected in the most sensual way possible. Without speaking a word, they both immediately knew what the other person was thinking and feeling. Brandi was sitting on the bed while Blake sat on the chair. With both their eyes locked on each other, Blake rose up from the chair and walked over to the bed and grabbed Brandi by her left hand. Brandi instantly became nervous and anxious at the same time. As Blake grabbed Brandi's hand, Brandi stood up and they both stood there as if they could see into each other's soul. Their faces were so close that the tips of their noses were touching. They both could feel the intense emotions of the other. They stood there and looked at each other for what felt like eternity.

It was as if they were making passionate love, it was like being in a dream; however, this was really happening. After gazing at each other for several minutes, Blake leaned and kissed Brandi ever so gently that she really thought this had to be a dream, Blake's kiss made Brandi's body almost lifeless, she could barely keep her legs from giving way. Blake's kiss was one of the fantasy kisses that little girls dream about when they think about a princess being kissed for the very first time by her prince. Not only did this kiss make Brandi's "kitty kat" wet, it was throbbing and on the verge of exploding into the best orgasm of her life. Brandi felt her body going where it had never gone before and didn't know what to do, she was truly afraid and excited at the same time. Brandi had never felt these feelings before in her life. "What is happening to me, is this what real love and passion feels like?" she thought to herself.

Ricco and Blue arrived at the hotel and noticed Brandi's car parked in the garage. Ricco didn't know what kind of car Blake drove, even though it's parked next to Brandi's. Ricco and Blue decided to wait in the garage until Black arrived and work on a plan to get rid of Blake, Preach and possibly Brandi.

While Ricco and Blue were working on the plan, Tiffany pulled into the garage where she saw Blake's car. She knew right away that he was in the hotel. Her assumption was that Ricco was there to do a drug deal with him and Preach and then have them killed. Tiffany was still trying to put the "why" into the equation, because so far, things were not adding up.

Tiffany made a call to Blake to see if she could get some information out of him about where he was and what he was up to. "Hey honey, what's up with you today?" asked Tiffany. "Not much, about to go into a meeting, what's up with you?" asked Blake. "Just missing you this morning and needed to hear your voice," said Tiffany. "I'm missing you as well. I know I've been a little distant lately, I have so much on my mind and have been trying to sort everything out," said Blake. "Like what?" asked Tiffany. "I can't get into it right now but I will share my thoughts with you very soon, just give me a minute to figure things out," said Blake. "What are you talking about?" asked Tiffany. "As I said, I will tell you, just can't get into it right now, okay" said Blake. "Okay honey bunch, I'm here whenever you're ready to talk, I love you Blake, no matter what, just remember that," said Tiffany. "I love you even more" said Blake. After they hung up the phone, Tiffany grabbed her black bag and headed into the hotel.

Shortly thereafter, Black pulled into the garage and parked next to Ricco and Blue. Black got out of his car and got into the truck where the two were talking. Ricco went over the plan with Blue and Black and the three got out of the SUV and went inside the hotel. Ricco had instructed Black to take the stairs to the 7th floor and wait on his signal to move. He also had Blue take the opposite staircase in the hotel to the 7th floor and wait on his instructions. Tiffany noticed Ricco when he entered the hotel lobby and followed him onto the elevator. Ricco pressed the 7th floor button and asked Tiffany what floor, she told him she was going to the same floor. While on the elevator, Ricco was admiring how beautiful she was and started a small conversation with her. "It must be hard to look so beautiful this early in the morning," said Ricco. "Thanks for the compliment, but it's not as hard as you think," said Tiffany. "Well tell your husband he is a lucky man," said Ricco. "I will do just that when I get one," said Tiffany. "You must be kidding, I can't believe some man has not captured you," said Ricco. "I didn't say I didn't have a man, I just said I don't have a husband," said Tiffany. The elevator door opened and Ricco being a gentleman, let Tiffany walked out first.

Tiffany didn't know in which direction to walk, she was hoping it was the opposite way from where Ricco was going so she could figure out the room number. As Tiffany made the left out of the elevator, Ricco also made the left but stopped immediately at the first door. Tiffany took a small makeup mirror out of her purse so she could see what Ricco was doing. Ricco stood in front of the door but turned around as if he was looking for someone down the hallway. As Tiffany kept walking down the hall, she stopped at the last door just before the exit stairway and knock on the door. Blue, by now was coming down the hall towards Ricco, as he was still standing at the door. Tiffany figured that was the room where everything would go down. As Blue was about to pass the elevator and be right next to Ricco, the elevator door opened and a housekeeper came out. Just as she came out Ricco knocked on the door and when the housekeeper saw him, she asked whether he was looking for the guest who had occupied that room; his response was in the affirmative. She told Ricco that she saw that guest on the elevator, and she got off on the second floor. Ricco asked her if she knew the room number because he was looking for his wife to surprise her for their anniversary. The housekeeper told Ricco she didn't know what room she went to. Ricco asked her if she could find out because of the gift that was arriving at the hotel within the next 30 minutes. Ricco told the housekeeper it would be a disaster if it were to be delivered to the wrong room. The housekeeper told him to stay where he was and allow her time to get the information. Ricco handed her $50 for being so kind, and he asked her to keep it on the down low to not ruin the surprise.

Tiffany heard the entire conversation and headed to the exit at the end of the hall to go down the stairs. The moment she opened the door, she saw a big black dude in a leather jacket and black gloves; she knew right away he was one of Ricco's henchmen. Tiffany passed him as he waited in the stairway and started going down the steps. As Tiffany was going down the steps she reached into her black bag and pulled out a 9mm silencer, turned before she got to the last step and shot Black in the back twice. Tiffany immediately pulled him down the stairs onto the 6th floor where no one was visible. She stashed him in the utility closet. Being aware of the trail of blood in the stairway, Tiffany went to the utility closet and got herself a bottle of bleach and towels. Tiffany took several towels and cleaned up all the blood in the stairway. Afterwards, Tiffany went down the stairs to the lobby to figure things out. Moments later the housekeeper came back and told Ricco she could not find out where on the 2nd floor his wife went; Ricco graciously thanked her for her efforts. He sent Blue to the other exit to tell Black to meet them on the second floor, but to stay in the stairway. Blue went to the other stairway to deliver the message to Black. Blue came back to Ricco at the elevator and told him that he didn't see Black in the stairway. Ricco was puzzled why Black was not in the stairway and more importantly, where the hell was he? Preach, Gary and one of their crew (Jake) arrived at the hotel. Preach gave them a heads up on the ride that things may get crazy if Ricco figured out what Blake and Brandi were up to, so everyone needed to be on the lookout for anything suspicious.

Tiffany had made her way to the second floor hoping to find out what room Blake and Brandi were staying. When she arrived from the stairway and onto the floor, she noticed a housekeeper going to one of the rooms with some items in her hand. As Blake and Brandi continued getting intimate, there was a knock at the door. "Who is it?" asked Blake. "House Keeping," a voice responded. "Yes, I ordered some condiments from the front desk, I forgot to pack a toothbrush and deodorant," said Brandi. Blake got up to answer the door because Brandi's shirt and Bra was completely off at this point.

Tiffany happened to see the housekeeper leaving the room after delivering the condiments and stopped her in the hallway. "Excuse me, my boyfriend switched out our room due to problems from the previous room but I forgot the room number. I know you're not supposed to give out guest's information, but, was the person who answered the door a 6 foot 2 gorgeous looking black man? Please say yes so I don't have to go all the way to the front desk and come back," said Tiffany. "Yes madam, that's exactly who answered the door, I think he is getting ready for you, he had no shirt on," said the housekeeper. "Thank you so much, you saved me a trip back downstairs," said Tiffany. Tiffany now knows what room Blake was in, but was puzzled as to why he had his shirt off. Tiffany headed to the front desk and asked the front desk clerk if room 204 or 208 was available for rent. The clerk told her that room 208 was available; Tiffany rented room 208. Meanwhile Tiffany was checking into room 208, Ricco had reached the second floor, but there was no sign of Blake or Brandi. The floor was completely empty and quiet. Ricco thought for a second and decided to go to the lobby to regroup and figure out what the hell happened to Black. As Ricco headed downstairs, Tiffany was heading upstairs to room 208. Tiffany entered her room, she immediately unloaded her black bag which had multiple electronic surveillance and listening gadgets. She removed a small wire type device and stuck it under the joining door between the two rooms so she could hear what was going on in the room Blake occupied. Tiffany started listening and was surprised that a woman was in the room with Blake.

She could hear them talking about how much they cared for each other. Tiffany wasnow in total oblivion. She thought Blake was caught up in a potential drug deal with someone who wanted to kill him. Now, her head was spinning out of control about what was going on. Preach, Gary and Jake entered the hotel lobby. Preach went to an in-house phone to call Blake to let him know they were at the hotel and he was coming up. Tiffany heard Blake talking on the phone to Preach. She also heard Blake tell Brandi to put on her bra and shirt because Preach was on his way. While Preach was making the call on the house phone, Ricco happened to see him, but Preach didn't see Ricco. Ricco saw Preach heading for the elevator and immediately headed to the stairway with Blue. Ricco and Blue ran up the stairs to the 2nd floor. They saw Preach got off the elevator and headed to a room three doors down. Ricco watched as Preach knocked on the door and entered the room.

Blake opened the door while Brandi sat on the edge of the bed. "What the fuck is going on nephew? Seems like everything you planned got totally messed up," said Preach. "I know, I know. The worst part is that now Ricco knows that we were setting him up to go to jail and that Brandi is in on everything with us. That's why I switched the rooms just to be safe. I'm starting to think that he may have had someone following Brandi," said Blake. "What the fuck! So nephew, you know there is a chance Ricco might be here at the hotel waiting on an opportunity to kill all of us," said Preach. "That's very possible at this point," said Blake. "Look, we need to get the hell out of this hotel and get somewhere safe. I have a safe spot that no one knows about in Southwest, DC. It's secluded and we can see anyone coming from all directions," said Preach. "That sounds perfect. You now got me wondering if Ricco is here at the hotel," said Blake. "I didn't see him in the lobby and Gary and Jake are down there on the lookout. If Gary spotted Ricco, trust me, we would hear gunshots immediately. Tell you what nephew, I'm going to get the car and pull it around to the front of the hotel, I want you and Brandi to meet me there in 15 minutes. I'm going to stop at the lobby and make sure Ricco and his crew are not around," said Preach.

Ricco watched Preach leave the room and got on the elevator. At this moment, Ricco and Blue headed for the hotel door where Blake and Brandi were staying. There is a knock at the door, Blake was in the restroom taking a leak, he yelled to Brandi "Preach must have forgotten to tell us something else; can you open the door?" Brandi opened the door and is surprised by Ricco and Blue. Ricco pushed Brandi back from the door and at this moment, Blake came from the restroom. Blue had a gun with a silencer in his hand and told Blake not to move or make a sound or he would kill him. Brandi backed up in fear as she noticed the gun in Ricco's hand as well. Blake immediately grabbed Brandi, "What do you want with us?" asked Blake. "US, fuck you mean US? ... That's my motherfucking wife you're holding onto and you talking about US. You must be out of your fucking mind to think you could bring me down and take my woman. All I can say for you youngster is that you must have some huge balls; doesn't matter though, because you are about to die. Before you die Blake, I need you to answer a few questions for me. Firstly, where is my fucking money? Secondly, how long have you been fucking my wife? Take your time and answer carefully, her life depends on it," said Ricco.

Ricco had Blue tie Blake to the chair with belts from the two robes in the closet and the iron cord. Ricco had a verbally abusive conversation with Brandi about fucking someone while being married to him. Brandi politely reminded him of the kids he produced during their marriage and the countless women he had probably been with; and the fact that he is a drug dealer. Tiffany heard what was being said in the room by Ricco. Tiffany now knows that Blake and Brandi are in the room and from what she could hear; she thought they may have been having sex in the room before Ricco showed up. Based on her 'intel' from Mike (DEA), she knows that Brandi and Blake went to college together, but didn't see any connection after college in the records received.

Tiffany changed from her work clothes to a black jumpsuit, which had a bullet proof vest on the inside, black leather boots, and a black baseball cap with black sunglasses. It was the type of gear Green Beret special operations members wore when they were on a covert mission. Tiffany knew she had to move quickly in order to save Blake. She went to her hotel room balcony and jumped across to the balcony where Blake and Brandi were. Tiffany could now see inside the room and heard what was being said. Tiffany saw Ricco and saw that Blue had Blake tied to a chair and Brandi was sitting on the couch in the room looking afraid. Ricco kept asking Blake how long was he fucking Brandi which Blake denied ever happened. Ricco was so angry at Blake's response that he smacked him in the face with the gun he had in his hand. The impact of the hit made the chair fall backwards and Tiffany could now see Blake's face was bloody from the blow; Brandi pleaded with Ricco to stop hitting Blake. "Aw, you want to protect your boyfriend now! This is the man who tried to destroy my business and take my wife and you want me to have mercy on him?" asked Ricco. "Please don't hurt him Ricco, I beg you, Please", said Brandi. "Do you love this motherfucker?" asked Ricco. Brandi didn't answer, she just sat there crying.

"Boss, what do you want to do, kill both of them?" asked Blue. "I'm still trying to decide, but first I want to know where my fucking money is. Let me find out just how much he loves you. "Blue, put your gun to Blake's head and let me ask my questions again," said Ricco. "Now Mr. Blake, where is my money, where is Preach and are you in love with my wife?" asked Ricco. Blake just sat there and wouldn't say a word which further pissed Ricco - something terrible. "Oh, so neither one of you feel like talking now, okay, I know just how to fix that problem," said Ricco.

At that moment, the room door opened and Preach came in with guns in both hands. Blue immediately grabs Blake around the neck and holds his gun against Blake's head. Ricco immediately jumped and grabbed Brandi around the neck and held his gun to her head. "Well, well, well, what do we have here, why didn't someone invite me to the party, I could have at least brought some Doritos or something!" said Preach.

"Always the jokester, said Ricco"

"I'm giving you and your nephew 10 seconds to tell me where my money is or Blue will blow his head clean off," said Ricco. "You know something Ricco, I thought you were a better man than this, real hustlers never allow personal things to get in the way of business," said Preach.

"Motherfucker, you were the one who probably orchestrated your nephew hooking up with my wife to infiltrate my business. Where is my fucking money?" asked Ricco.

"I got your money you piece of shit," said Preach. At that moment, a shot rang through the balcony window breaking the glass and hitting Blue in the back of the head, as he was falling to the ground he squeezed a shot that hit Preach in the shoulder causing him to hit the floor but kept his guns pointed at Ricco.

Everyone in the room was shocked, trying to figure out who took that shot and why. Slowly, Tiffany entered the hotel room with her gun pointed at Ricco. "Who the fuck are you?" asked Ricco. "I'm the answer to all your problems," said Tiffany. "You don't know me lady," said Ricco. "To the contrary, I know you extremely well. I know you're married to this beautiful young lady you're choking. I know you have a dental practice which is a front for your drug business. I know you have a set of twin kids in Florida and a son in Washington, DC. I know you have been one of the biggest drug dealers in the Washington DC area for the past 20 years; should I continue," asked Tiffany.

Blake and Preach were looking at Tiffany in total amazement. "So Ricco, how do want to play this out, you let this young lady go and live or die on the spot?" asked Tiffany "I'm leaving out of here with her and if anyone tries to stop me, a bullet will go through her brain before I hit the ground," said Ricco. Ricco started backing toward the door with Brandi tightly secured in his left arm and the gun pressed against her temple with his right hand.

"Let him go Preach" said Tiffany. "No, he will kill her first chance he gets," said Blake. "We got this, just let him go," said Tiffany. Ricco backed out of the hotel room into the hallway with Brandi in tow. "Who the hell is we?" asked Blake. "I got this, just trust me," said Tiffany. "Who are you?" asked Blake. "I'm your fiancé, remember" said Tiffany with a smile on her face. "We gotta talk," said Blake. "Yes we do, but right now, let me handle my business," said Tiffany.

Tiffany pulled out a police looking radio from the back of her vest. "Mike, Tiff here, go ahead - make the call. "What the fuck is going on Tiffany?" asked Blake. "Baby boy, I got you," said Tiffany. Preach is looking at Blake trying to figure out who the hell is this Tiffany and what the hell is going on. Blake looked at Preach with the same puzzled look. Tiffany went to Preach, helped him off the floor and took a look at his wound. "You'll be fine, the bullet went straight through the shoulder," said Tiffany. Both Preach and Blake were looking at Tiffany with total confusion. "Nephew, who is your fiancé?" asked Preach. "I'm not sure Preach, I'm not sure," said Blake.

Ricco took Brandi down the stairway to the garage to Brandi's car. Ricco realized that he didn't have keys to the SUV that Blue used to pick him up and he still didn't know where Black was, so his only option was to take Brandi's car. However, once he reached Brandi's car and opened the door, a phone was sitting on the driver's seat. The phone rang and Ricco answered it "Yea." "Listen closely, I will give you one opportunity to get out of here, a key is in the ignition for your convenience; you let the girl go and drive away, if not, you will go to jail for attempted murder and kidnapping and spend the next 30 years in a federal prison. Your choice… choose wisely," said the voice on the phone.

Ricco took one last look at Brandi and said" IT AIN'T OVER"!!

Milton Keynes UK
Ingram Content Group UK Ltd.
UKHW030238030224
437175UK00001B/43